PIN

AN MC ROMANCE (OUTLAW SOULS BOOK 2)

HOPE STONE

© Copyright 2020 - All rights reserved.

It is not legal to reproduce, duplicate, or transmit any part of this document in either electronic means or in printed format. Recording of this publication is strictly prohibited and any storage of this document is not allowed unless with written permission from the publisher except for the use of brief quotations in a book review.

This book is a work of fiction. Any resemblance to persons, living or dead, or places, events or locations is purely coincidental.

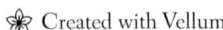 Created with Vellum

OUTLAW SOULS MEMBERS
MEMBERSHIP ROSTER

President
Paul "Padre" Padillo
Vice President
Robert "Ryder" Hernandez
SGT at Arms
Susie "Swole" Holt
Road Captain
Raul "Trainer" Lopez
Secretary
Open
Treasurer
Gabriel "Pin" Gallegos
Enforcer
Michael "The Moves" Jagger
Prospects
Kimberly Delasante
Carlos Brown
Patches
Pedro "Hawk" Sanchez

Diego "The Dog" Christopher
Vlad "The Enforcer" Kushniruk
Robbie "Chalupa" Iglesias
Chaplain
Ming "Yoda" Chi

ONE
PIN

"Alright, brothers, that's it for me," Ryder said.

I looked up from my bike to see Ryder standing up and brushing off his dark jeans. He nodded at Moves and me as he headed for the door. We had been working on our bikes at the shop for the last hour or so like we did almost every Friday afternoon.

"Aw, you're really blowing us off for drinks again?" Moves asked.

"Yeah, I'm sick of dragging your drunk ass home every night," Ryder snapped.

I smirked down at the ground. I loved it when Moves and Ryder badgered each other. They never meant any harm. It was all in good fun, just one of the things that made us brothers, bonded by our devotion to our club, the Outlaw Souls.

"Pin, I'll see ya later," Ryder said.

He clapped my shoulder as he headed out, his back ramrod straight. Ryder was the type of guy who thought he had to carry the whole world on his shoulders. It showed sometimes in the way he walked with purpose and a hint of weariness.

Once the roar of his motorcycle had faded into the distance, Moves glanced at me. "You're coming to Blue Dog Saloon, right?"

"Wouldn't miss it," I said.

Moves was the enforcer of our group. He had earned that position through a dedication to street fighting that was, frankly, terrifying. Nearly every day, I thanked my lucky stars that he was on our side.

As enforcer, Moves always liked to be in the thick of things, and he never missed a meet-up among club members. It was Friday, so that meant drinks and music down at the Blue Dog Saloon, our unofficial headquarters.

The bar was located on the dingy side of La Playa, far away from the glistening sandy beaches and the boardwalk. Blue Dog Saloon was scrappy but proud, just like the club itself.

"Sweet," Moves said. "Maybe this time you'll actually get a girl's number."

He grinned at me beneath his messy mop of sandy brown hair.

I rolled my eyes. It wasn't that I couldn't get a woman, it was just that I only liked having one for a few nights. I wasn't into all that soul-changing all-consuming type of love. Moves was, but somehow he could never find it. He was always getting his heart broken or breaking someone else's heart and then breaking some noses as well, just to round everything out.

"You don't mean that," I said. "You'd be screwed without my wingman skills."

As I stood up, Moves jokingly shoved me in the chest. I dodged away with a laugh, but patted my chest to make sure my glasses were in one piece. Moves had already broken my accounting glasses three times in the last six months and I was sick of getting replacements.

I had been the treasurer for Outlaw Souls for over three years. I kept my glasses on me at all times in case I needed to crunch numbers at any point. We always had gigs, odd jobs, and fundraisers, so keeping track of all the influx and outflow was no joke.

I was happy to do it though; the club was everything to me. I had been born and raised on the wrong side of La Playa. Sick of my mom's non-stop fighting with her boyfriend, I had joined up as soon as I was eighteen. I was never the guy to grab the center of attention, so I had always wanted to be treasurer – not in the middle of things, but still pulling strings behind-the-scenes.

I remembered when the older guys had suggested I get an accounting degree at a local college, I'd been almost offended. I thought they were trying to get rid of me or hint that I wasn't suited for a biker club. Instead, they explained that they needed someone with certain skills and, since I had done so well in high school math courses, I had potential.

I had done well in math because it was a good distraction from whatever jerk my mom was seeing that month, but I didn't tell them that. Instead, I got into an accounting program with the club paying for the whole thing. They didn't ask for a single penny back. That's when I knew I would do anything for the Outlaw Souls. It's been almost ten years since I first asked to join, and I feel the same way.

I grabbed my leather jacket with the patch and pulled it on as Moves gathered up his stuff. He looked at his phone and then up at me. "Kimmy just texted, she's headed that way as well."

I rolled my eyes. Kimberly Delasante was a pledge who hated – absolutely hated – being called "Kimmy." So, of course, Moves called her nothing else. Kim was a tough girl though, and always gave as good as she got with Moves.

Moves and I pushed our bikes out into the bright sun of La Playa. It would start to set soon, so we had just enough time to go for a quick ride and grab dinner before heading to Blue Dog.

The auto shop we liked to work out of was on the corner across from a rundown taco place and a loan's office. The taco place needed a serious paint job and had grimy windows, but we all knew that they were the best tacos outside LA. There was another, shinier version of La Playa, but it wasn't for me, never had been.

"Seriously, man, I worry about you," Moves said as the sun hit us.

It was pretty out of the blue, so I raised my brows.

"You got walls a mile high, brother," Moves continued. "Being single is fun for a while, but come on, you don't wanna be grabbing beers with your brothers every Friday for the rest of your life, right?"

To be honest, I kinda did, but I wasn't going to admit that to Moves. Beneath his battle-hardened exterior, he was a total romantic. He believed in soulmates and all that bullshit.

I wasn't going to be the one to tell him that true love didn't exist.

Because it didn't. I had known that since I was five years old and my dad walked out, leaving my mom weeping on the floor of our shitty little kitchen.

I hadn't seen my dad since. Hadn't wanted to. Even when Ryder and Moves suggested I try tracking him down, for closure, I wasn't having it. Some stones are better left unturned.

Not to mention that while I didn't have many memories of him, I had enough to know he wasn't worth knowing. I remember waking up to his drunken ranting late at night, and I remember him constantly losing a job but blaming someone else for his unemployment. It was never his fault. His boss was always a prick, or his friend threw him under the bus, or my mother was such a nag and drove him crazy.

My mother loved him, she really did. But that never did her any good, just made her hurt all the more when he betrayed her. Unfortunately, my mom fell in love easily. She fell in love with the next guy, and the next, and the next. And she always ended up crying with her broken heart in her hands.

The truth was, people weren't good enough for each other. One way or another, someone always cheated or walked out or lied. So I was happy to flirt and engage in the occasional fuck, but why bother with anything else?

I wanted my life to be like the numbers on my accounting books. Even, balanced. No lies. No evasions. No room for slip-ups.

Moves shrugged at my silence. He was used to it. I had never been much of a talker.

"Still waters run deep," Moves mumbled.

I pushed my sunglasses on as we mounted our bikes.

"What about Kimmy?" Moves blurted out. "She's cute, right?"

I snorted. Moves had never been subtle. Also, I was pretty sure he was the one with a thing for Kim, he just didn't know it yet.

"Definitely not my type," I said. "Besides, she's seeing someone."

"She is?" Moves asked.

"Yeah, I heard her telling Carlos about it the other day," I said. "Older guy, I think. Big corporate job, sounds like."

"Fuck," Moves said. "I guess someone is willing to risk getting close to that bitch on wheels."

I rolled my eyes at Moves' ever-changing opinions. The guy had more mood swings than a teenage girl. "You just said she was cute."

"Yeah, well," Moves said. "I say a lotta things."

I pushed my dark hair back from my face and rammed my boot down on the pedal. I was getting sick of chit-chat, even if Moves mostly meant well.

Moves started revving his own engine and our bikes roared to life.

As we hit the open road, I couldn't hold back my grin. We merged onto the highway and headed south. If we were to go straight west, we would hit the ocean. That was one of my favorite rides, but we didn't have time.

I leaned forward and urged my bike even faster. The feeling of the wind pulsing over my face as my bike picked up speed was what I had fallen in love with first. The club and the brotherhood had just been added bonuses.

I figured between my bike and my brothers, who needed anything else?

TWO
CLAIRE

I tossed the envelope onto Veronica's desk with a dramatic sigh. "Men are idiots."

"Tell me about it," Veronica said, not even looking up as I flopped into my desk chair.

"This guy was legit emailing his mistress naked pics from his personal phone that is part of his family plan, which his wife is on," I said. "She gave me all the passwords so logging on was a breeze. She could have done it herself."

"Claire, baby, they *never* want to do it themselves," Veronica said. "It's easier if we swoop in and find the dirty stuff for them."

I shrugged and kicked my feet up on the desk. When I had first landed the job at Daniel O'Malley's private investigating firm, I had been excited. Following cheating husbands with big sunglasses and a fancy camera had been thrilling.

But after three years, it was getting old. I could practically recite the result of every case brought to us by some weeping wife.

Her bigwig husband had a mistress, who was probably

under twenty-five and had massive tits. He thought he was so clever by using a burner phone and telling his wife he had to work late. We usually only had to trail the husband for a few days before we could get back to the wife with photos, emails, texts, and other pieces of evidence that her divorce attorney would know how to use.

Occasionally, there was something a little more riveting. Sometimes a missing child, a guy who owed money and was trying to disappear, or even a murder that the police couldn't crack. But for the most part, it was asshole husbands.

Veronica swung her thick dark hair over one shoulder and gave me a wry smile. "Think Dan got another one in today. It'll go to you though. I'm not done working on this one."

I raised my eyebrows. Veronica usually sped through her cases. While I preferred to trail the guys and gather evidence off of phones or hard drives, Veronica did it the old-fashioned way. She'd put on an itty-bitty black dress and waltz right up to the scumbag at the bar. A few hours later, she would be in his hotel room, plenty of photos taken for the poor wife, and lecturing the guy on being an idiot.

"You're kidding," I said. "This guy said no to you?"

"He's a careful one," Veronica said. "Doesn't drink either, which is always a challenge."

"You'll get him," I said.

"I always do," Veronica said with a wicked gleam in her eye.

Veronica and I were the only two employees who worked for Dan. She had been at the firm for almost a decade and had pretty much taught me everything I knew.

I had been green when I arrived in La Playa with twenty

bucks in my wallet and a thirst for adventure. I had wanted to try being a stunt double in Hollywood or a personal assistant for a millionaire. Anything that would offer adventure really.

I grew up in a small town in Northern California. My parents were nice, but ordinary. By the time I graduated from the local college, I was desperate for something new and exciting. So I headed south and never looked back.

Working as a PI was exciting. It was. I loved the life I had created for myself in La Playa. But lately, I had been chomping at the bit for something else. A bigger case. A new challenge.

"You ok?" Veronica asked.

She was observant, that's part of what made her a great PI. She had noticed my sense of ennui.

"Sure," I said with a small shrug. "Just bored."

"If you're always looking for the next thrill," Veronica said. "You'll miss all the good things you've got."

"Thanks, Yoda."

Beneath her femme fatale exterior, Veronica was wise and sympathetic. She was the uncontested best at breaking the tough news to the wives of the cheaters. I was always too abrupt. I would just shove the photos in their face, telling them the man they had been married to for years sucked and they needed to move on fast.

Veronica was more understanding. She held a lot of hands, wiped away a lot of tears, and gave amazing pep talks about how this wasn't the end, it was a new beginning. I knew that if I ever got gutted by a cheating husband, I would run to Veronica first.

Not like that would ever happen though. After the bullshit I had seen in the last few years, long-term relationships looked about as appealing as a dumpster fire to me. Besides, every guy I dated ended up boring me. I always got tired of the same old routines.

The door swung open and Daniel O'Malley strutted into the office. He was over six feet tall, his suits were always wrinkled, and his hair was always messy, but he had managed to build a successful private investigating business over the course of two decades. He said it was because he had always hired smart and capable girls like me and Veronica.

I swung my feet off my desk and straightened my oversized jean jacket.

"Fenelli," he barked at Veronica. "Still working the Greenberg guy?"

"Yup," Veronica said.

"Brennan?" he asked, turning to me.

Daniel always used our last names. I think it made him feel like he was in an old-school Hollywood detective movie.

"Finished with the latest today," I said. "Just need to type up the report."

"Great," Daniel said, tossing a file onto my desk. "I've got a new one."

I opened it up. Olivia Cook was concerned by her husband Trey's recent behavior. She wanted to get to the bottom of it, as painful as the truth may be. I scanned the pictures. Olivia looked like something out of Town & Country magazine. Blonde hair, big smile, floral dress, cute kid clinging to her hand.

Trey also looked the part. Handsome face and a build that suggested he had been an athlete in high school but was just starting to go to seed a bit. Guys like that gained a few pounds, got a few gray hairs, and their fragile masculinity exploded. They had to go out and shower some dumb young bimbo with gifts to get their self-esteem back on track.

"Wonderful," I said. "Another thrilling chapter in the book of matrimonial bliss."

Veronica stifled a giggle, but Daniel frowned.

"Let's 86 the sarcasm, Brennan," Daniel said.

I flashed him my most charming smile. "Sure thing, boss. I'll get right on this tonight."

Daniel gave a brisk nod and headed into his office. He gave off a stern exterior, but he was a good guy overall.

I settled into my desk and pulled out my notebook. My desk was a mess of papers, photos, and pens, but I thrived in that kind of disarray. Veronica, on the other hand, kept her desk immaculate.

Two hours later, I had finished putting together my final report. I sent it to Daniel and then grabbed the next file. As tired as I was with the cheating husbands, I always got a little thrill of anticipation with a new case. It was like a wrapped present where you *thought* you knew what it was, but you couldn't be sure.

Anything could lurk beneath the shining veneer of Trey and Olivia Cook. It could be scandal, intrigue, a web of deceit that stretched back years. He could be the head of a coke ring or the leader of some crazy cult. No matter what it was, I, Claire Brennan, would crack the case.

It was probably just a mistress with big tits. But it could be something else, and that's what gave me the little flutter of butterflies in my stomach.

I read over the info about Trey's office and license plate number. I checked my watch. If I hustled, I might be able to trail him as he left his work. It was Friday night, so if he was meeting his side chick, it would be about now while his wife was at home making mac and cheese for the kid.

I shoved the file into my bag and stood up.

"Heading out already?" Veronica asked.

"Might as well," I said. "Who knows? This one could be different."

Veronica smirked. "Maybe."

Fifteen minutes later, I was parked outside his office in the heart of La Playa near the boardwalk. He had a nice cushy position in a consulting firm; probably had a corner office too.

I rolled down my window and kept my eye on his car. When I first started the whole PI thing, my instinct was to do it like the movies. Big sunglasses, a hat, maybe even a scarf. But the secret to not being seen is to not try and hide. Just dawdle about in plain sight. Look like you're up to absolutely nothing.

It doesn't hurt that no one suspects foul play from the petite girl with a blonde ponytail.

Veronica does it a little differently. She wants to be seen. She wants the guy to notice her so much that he can't resist. Not me. I stick to my corners where I can watch undetected.

At six on the dot, Trey Cook strolled out of his office and hopped into his car. In the distance, the sun was setting over the water. He was working late for a Friday, but maybe he did that to cover his bases if his wife ever asked a coworker.

If I were a betting woman, I would have put my money on Trey heading straight to one of the bougie cocktail bars or steakhouses in downtown La Playa. Mistresses loved that kind of thing while men like Trey loved to impress.

It's a good thing I didn't gamble, because Trey surprised me by driving all the way out to East La Playa.

"Ok, Trey," I muttered. "We're roughing it tonight."

He finally pulled up to a bar I had never been to called *Blue Dog Saloon*. It didn't look dangerous, per se, but it was decidedly shabby. Not without charm, though.

I cast a wary eye towards the bikes parked outside. There were biker clubs all around LA, but I had never had any trouble with them. Then again, I had never really gone near bikers.

Overall, it was not the type of bar I expected Trey to frequent. This case was looking more interesting by the second.

I looked down at myself. I was wearing worn black jeans with frayed hems, sturdy boots, and my reliable jean jacket. Not exactly a Friday Night Out Look, but any PI worth her salt is always prepared for wardrobe adjustments.

I pulled my hair out of its ponytail and ran my hands through it until it settled in soft waves down to my shoulders. Then I dug around in my bag and yanked out some dark red lipstick and mascara.

After hastily applying the makeup, I shoved my wallet and my phone into my smaller handbag. It looked weird to walk into a bar with a huge tote bag. Getting pictures would be tricky, even if I used my phone instead of my nicer camera.

I shoved my small pink pepper spray into my purse as well. I was pretty street-smart and I knew how to avoid risky situations, but a girl could never be too careful.

At the last minute, I tugged my jean jacket off. I was wearing a white lacy blouse with short sleeves, cropped to show just an inch of my stomach. If I needed to flirt my way around the bar that would help.

Veronica had taught me how to keep everything I might need for any venue in my car. She also always had at least three pairs of heels, but I skipped that step. I never wore heels. They made it too hard to run if things got dicey.

I pulled myself out of the car and walked towards the entrance. There was a cute hanging sign of a blue dog with rock music blasting from within. I burned with curiosity. What was Trey up to?

Once inside, it didn't take me long to figure it out. I casually scanned the room as I headed towards the bar and spotted him right away. In his button-down shirt and tie, he stood out like a sore thumb.

He was holding hands with a drop-dead gorgeous woman. She had legs for days and raven-black hair. I blinked in surprise when I saw she wasn't in the typical Mistress Fashion. She was wearing a black leather jacket and jeans, introducing Trey to a few guys who wore matching leather jackets.

I felt a pang of sympathy. I bet she didn't even know the jerk had a wife. Most of the mistresses were aware of a wife, they just don't care or they think he'll leave her someday. Sometimes they honestly don't know, and those were always tough.

This girl looked way too self-respecting to be with a married guy. It was unlikely she knew.

I leaned on a chair and waited for the people in front of me to finish ordering. I furrowed my brow as I tried to come up with a plan of action. Snapping photos was risky in a bar since people would notice.

Plus, Olivia would want more than a few blurry pictures. It's amazing how wives, even the smart ones, can justify damning photo evidence. They needed it to be undeniable before they believed their beloved husbands have betrayed them. I would need to trail Trey a bit more, and maybe dig up some texts.

I could also try and approach the girl on her own. It was risky, and it sometimes backfired to enlist the mistress, but it could pay off. Especially if she had a taste for revenge. I glanced back at the tall beauty and observed her flashing eyes. Definitely looked like the revenge type.

"Hey, can I get you a drink?"

I stifled an eye roll as I turned around at the masculine voice. Then blinked in surprise when I saw a leather jacket beneath a cocky grin. The same leather jacket Trey's side piece was wearing. What a delightful surprise. I could see the patch on the arm now. Outlaw Souls.

I gave him a sweet smile and shrugged. "I'll take a Corona."

Within minutes, the biker had gotten both of us a beer. He had to know the bartender.

"I'm Claire," I said.

"Pleasure," he said. "I'm Moves."

He jerked his head and led me back towards his friends. I took a deep breath. It was beyond risky interacting with the person you were trailing too early in the game. Veronica never put on her itty-bitty dress until she had gathered all the information she needed.

Luckily, Trey had let the woman lead him out onto the dance floor while Moves was steering me towards a few of the guys perched at a table in the corner.

"Claire, this is Hawk and Carlos," Moves said. "And this is Pin."

I glanced at the guys as they nodded at me. They all had nicknames. I had heard biker clubs used alternate names, but I had always doubted it since it seemed a little cheesy.

Hawk and Carlos seemed nice and relaxed, but the third guy, Pin, looked like he had just swallowed a wasp. He clasped his lips together and barely gave me a nod. My eyes lingered on his broad shoulders and glowing tan skin before I turned back to Moves.

"So, you new in town?" Moves asked.

"No, I've been here a few years," I said. "I work in sales downtown."

My father used to say that I lied like a rug. Only he had told me it was a weakness. I had learned it was my greatest strength.

"What brings you out here?" Moves said.

"Meeting a friend," I said. "I'm just a bit early."

In fifteen minutes, I could glance at my phone and either say my friend had bailed or, if I needed an escape route, say she wanted to meet somewhere else and head for the exit.

I looked up at Moves just in time to see him widening his eyes at Pin and nodding at me. So Moves was the wingman for a very reluctant Pin. Interesting. I could work with that.

I pulled myself up into the chair next to Pin (where I still had a good angle on Trey and his girlfriend) and gave him a smile.

"So, *Pin*," I said. "How'd you get that name?"

THREE
PIN

I wanted to kill Moves. I wanted to knock him to the floor in the middle of the bar and beat the shit out of him. Being my wingman without my asking was one thing, but being a totally unsubtle wingman was borderline unforgivable.

All I had done was check out the cute blonde girl as she walked up to the bar when Moves had tracked my line of vision. Before I could stop him, he'd bolted towards her and brought her back. Now Claire probably thought I was a pathetic loser who needed my friend to pick up girls.

"So, *Pin*," she said, leaning on her elbows. "How'd you get that name?"

I blinked down at her. Her blonde hair hung in waving strands around her pert face. She was more than just cute. She was gorgeous. And something about the slant of her head made me think there was a lot of action going on behind her eyes. She had brains.

And the way she emphasized my name made me flush like an idiot.

I wasn't even looking to hook up tonight. I had no problem picking up girls when I wanted to and good at choosing the ones who also wanted nothing more than a hookup.

I had no idea what this girl wanted. Something about the way she had walked into the bar, sizing up the room as if she was on a mission, was mysterious to me. She wasn't easy to read.

"It's a long story," I said.

"Oh, well, never mind then," she said. "I hate long stories. They're usually pretty boring."

She raised her beer to her mouth and took a sip, keeping her eyes on me the whole time. I had the sudden urge to reach out and touch her rosy pink lips.

"It's not so boring," I said. "But I had better not risk your harsh judgment."

She laughed. "You're smart."

"Ah, she's got you pegged," Moves interjected. He turned to Claire. "He's the smartest guy in our club; that's why he's the treasurer and does all the accounting."

I rolled my eyes at Moves' blatant boasting. Why did he think accounting was sexy?

"Club?" Claire asked.

"We're a biker club," I said, nodding at my patch. "Outlaw Souls."

"Huh," she said.

She wasn't a biker chick, that was for certain.

"I've never met an accountant biker before," she said.

I raised my brows. She was definitely flirting with me. My stomach flipped with anticipation as I leaned closer to her. But my rational side told me to put the brakes on this soon.

Nothing about Claire said she was looking for a casual hook-up. Yes, she had accepted Moves' invitation, but she was also wearing minimal makeup, lowkey clothes, and flat-heeled shoes. Girls who came to the Blue Dog Saloon looking for sex were always dressed up a certain way. Low cut tops. Sky-high heels. Bronzer all over their face

Claire was barely showing any skin. Just a small strip of flat white stomach. And yeah, that was enticing, but overall her outfit indicated that she really did come here to meet a friend.

I had my rules for a reason. It was risky to fall hard for a girl like Claire. Way too risky. It would only lead to a messy heartbreak.

Her eyes flashed away from my face and over my shoulder. For a second, the lighthearted flirtatious look vanished and her eyes hardened into an almost predatory expression. I glanced over my shoulder and saw Kim and her new guy heading over. Maybe Claire didn't play well with other girls.

I looked back at her and wondered if I had imagined the flash of antagonism. Her face had smoothed over and she had a pleasant smile.

"Hey guys," Kim said. She plopped down in a chair, and I nodded at her.

"Kimmy!" Moves said with a large grin.

She rolled her eyes and looked up at Trey.

"I'll get us another round, babe," he said, heading towards the bar.

I had to admit, I was surprised by Trey. He seemed a polar opposite of Kim. He was certainly out of his element among us bikers, but it was kind of endearing that an office guy like him had come out to the Blue Dog Saloon for Kim.

"Hi, I'm Claire," Claire said.

Kim smiled and introduced herself.

"So you're a biker too, right?" Claire asked.

"Hell yeah," Kim said. "Or I will once I pledge."

"That's awesome," Claire said.

"Yeah, well, it may drive me insane," Kim said. "Especially if this one keeps calling me Kimmy."

She rolled her eyes at Moves, resulting in a heated back and forth between them.

Claire turned back to me. "How long have you been a biker?"

"Since I was sixteen," I said. "Joined when I was eighteen, so almost ten years."

I wasn't really focusing on my words. Instead, I was watching Claire's face to see if she got distracted again. Just when I thought I was being paranoid, her eyes flashed past me again. Right to Trey as he returned to the table with a drink for Kim.

So it was Trey she was watching. An ex possibly? Although surely one of them would have said something?

I shrugged and took a swig from my drink. It was stupid to obsess over this. I didn't want to pursue Claire, and she probably wasn't that interested in me anyway.

I paused to listen as Trey leaned closer to Kim to talk into her ear.

"Babe, I'm so sorry, but I gotta go," he said. "There's been a work emergency and I need to put something together for a client tonight."

Kim frowned, but she wasn't the type to whine. She didn't need her guy to have a good time on a Friday. "I understand. I'll see you tomorrow?"

"Of course," Trey said.

He said his goodbyes to the rest of us quickly and then headed out.

"Looks like we scared him off," Moves joked.

"As if," Kim said.

Moves finally succumbed to Kim's withering glare and

headed out to flirt with some girls he'd spotted across the bar. Carlos and Hawk wandered off as well so it was just me, Claire, and Kim.

To my surprise, Claire seemed more interested in getting to know Kim. She wasn't rude or anything, but as the conversation went on, she made an effort to ask Kim about her biking and how long she had been in La Playa. I was clearly not getting lucky tonight, but that was for the best. Claire was too enigmatic for my tastes.

She drummed her fingers on the table and leaned forward towards Kim.

"So how long have you been with –?" Claire waved her hand as if she couldn't recall the name. It was all almost too casual.

"Trey?" Kim said. "Just a few weeks."

"He seems nice," Claire said. She leaned forward as if she was ready to settle in for some serious girl talk. I guess I could comfort myself with the fact that I got to witness the start of a friendship.

"I'll be honest, he's not my usual type," Kim said. "But I like that he's actually an adult. I've dated too many Man-Children the last few years."

"Tell me about it," Claire said. "What does he do?"

"He works in consulting," Kim said. "And he travels a lot so his schedule is a little weird."

"That can work though," Claire said. "You don't strike me as the clingy type who needs to be with her guy 24/7."

"Oh, no way," Kim said with a laugh. "And he gets that. Like I said, he's an adult."

Claire nodded, and a pensive look drifted across her eyes.

"Although, Claire, not *all* biker guys are immature,"

Kim said, reaching over to brush a hand over my arm. "Pin here is definitely not of the Man-Child variety."

Kim threw Claire a wink, making Claire's cheeks turn red. She was adorable when she blushed. At least Kim was a better wingman than Moves.

"I got that sense," Claire said. "I've heard all about the legendary biker accountant."

"Best one in La Playa," Kim said.

"Hey, give me more credit than that," I said. "I'm at least the top in the LA greater area."

The conversation continued like that for a while. Claire was charming, I couldn't deny it. And I liked that she wasn't throwing herself at me. It made me want her even more.

But that was a bad idea.

When her drink was low, I stood up. "Should I grab us another round?"

"Yes, please," Kim said.

"Sure," Claire said.

Claire was a bad idea, but one more drink couldn't hurt?

FOUR
CLAIRE

Maybe it was the second beer, or maybe it was just that I really liked Kim, but I decided I had to come clean. Based on our conversation, I was 99% certain that Kim had no clue Trey had a wife.

I could also tell Kim was tough. She could handle the truth, especially since she and Trey had only been dating for a few weeks.

As for Pin, he was harder to nail down. With his dark hair and serious eyes, he was undeniably handsome, but he seemed reserved, like he was holding a large of himself back. I figured he was into me since Moves had been pretty obvious, but Pin wasn't exactly making any moves. Just a bit of flirtation, nothing more.

It didn't matter. I had no intention of going home with anyone and Pin was clearly Kim's friend. As long as Kim trusted him, I was fine with him.

I waited until Pin excused himself to go to the bathroom. Then I cut to the chase. I've always been direct.

"So I've got to confess," I said, looking Kim right in her

eyes. "I didn't come here tonight to meet a friend. I'm actually a private investigator."

Kim blinked and stiffened. "Sorry, what?"

"Trey is married, and his wife hired my firm to find proof of an affair," I said. "I'm guessing you didn't know, but you seem cool so I wanted to tell you the truth."

"Fuck," Kim said. "You're fucking kidding."

"I wish," I said with a grim smile. "But I can show you the file."

"Oh, no, I believe you," Kim said. "Honestly, I knew his whole wacky schedule was a bit weird – he never slept over at mine, and I sure as hell didn't get invited to his place."

"Yeah, that's pretty classic," I said. "In my line of work, we see a lot of this."

Kim pursed her lips and frowned down at her beer. It hurt to hear that you were being two-timed, but as I had predicted, Kim was not about to break down in tears. She did, however, look pissed.

"Ok, so tell me how I'm getting even," Kim said.

I gave her a devious grin. "I was hoping you would say that."

Pin returned to the table. He took one look at Kim, who almost had visible steam coming out of her ears and frowned. "So what did I just miss?"

I let Kim take the lead.

"That douchebag Trey is cheating on me," Kim said. "Or rather, he's cheating on his wife – Claire's a fucking PI hired to get proof."

I almost laughed aloud at Pin's shocked expression. His eyes widened and his mouth hung open. I needed to reveal myself in more of my cases, it was too fun.

"Sorry," I said. "I hate to be the bearer of bad news, but it's in my job description."

"No, you're badass," Kim said. "And we're gonna take that bastard down, right?"

"It's what I do best," I said. "But I'm gonna need some help from you."

"I'm so in," Kim said.

I nodded and hesitated.

"You're going to have to play nice with Trey for a little longer," I said. "Just to get him on another date where I can take photos and then, if you're comfortable, I would love to get some of the texts he's sent you?"

Kim looked upset at the idea of having to wait even a short period of time before letting Trey have it, but she nodded.

"Ok, wait a second," Pin interjected. "We just met, this is a lot to reveal, can we get some credentials or something?"

I raised one brow at him. He really was an accountant. An extremely well-muscled and deviously good-looking accountant.

"You're asking for my badge?" I asked. "PI's don't carry badges."

"Seriously, Pin, why would she lie?" Kim asked.

"I don't know, maybe she's Trey's ex or something," Pin said.

I scoffed. As if I would ever so much as touch trash like Trey Cook.

"I'm not saying I don't believe you," Pin said, holding up both of his hands. "I just think Kim deserves some concrete information before you guys go all Kill Bill."

Kim opened her mouth, but I held up my own hand. "Fair enough."

I pulled out my phone and quickly navigated to an article that had been written about Daniel O'Malley a few months ago. It had been a profile piece for the LA Times about an old missing person case Daniel had solved.

It featured a big photo of me, Daniel and Veronica posing in our offices. I handed my phone to Kim while Pin read over her shoulder.

"Shit," Kim said. "Y'all are the real deal."

I smiled with pride. Veronica had been unsure about having a photo. She thought it might interfere with cases if too many people recognized us. But in the end, we had been too excited about the article.

"Ok," Pin said. "I believe you."

"So kind of you," I said, my voice dripping with sarcasm.

Pin shrugged, but I saw a small smile tug at his mouth. I decided his caution was cute rather than annoying.

Kim recovered with remarkable speed. We finished our drinks while she enumerated all the times she should have seen right through Trey, yet oblivious as he was so doting and into her. But now, she knew better than to be blinded by a crush.

"Don't beat yourself up," I said. "Guys like Trey are master manipulators. Trust me, I deal with their wives and those women have been gaslighted all over the place."

I pursed my lips in disdain. Pin nodded along so quickly that I had to wonder if he had experience with a woman who had been manipulated. An old girlfriend maybe, or possibly a mother?

"She's right," Pin said. "At least you're not the wife sitting at home right now."

Kim shuddered and nodded. "So true. Is she – do you think she'll be ok?"

"I don't really know her," I said, considering how much to tell Kim. "But I'm sure she'll be fine. In my experience, these women always get the last laugh once their divorce attorney is done with their crummy husbands."

"Good," Kim said.

"I would not suggest you two meet though," I said as Kim nodded. "Too often the wives take it out on the mistresses. You'll be ok though. I get the sense you're pretty resilient."

"I've had to be," Kim said. "I swear, I have the worst luck in guys."

I gave her a sly grin and raised my glass. "Now that I understand."

I glanced at Pin just then, catching just the smallest quirk of his right eyebrow. It was a blink-and-you-miss-it movement, but I'm a PI. It's my job to never blink.

And the way he moved his eyebrow was as if he was responding to a challenge I'd put forth.

A half-hour later, I said my goodbyes. Kim and I had exchanged phone numbers and agreed on a tentative scheme that we would flesh out later.

Once I was back in my car, I chugged a bottle of water from my purse. Daniel would kill me if I got a DUI while on the job. I didn't feel tipsy though. I never drank too much when I was on a job, so I had been careful to only drink half of my second beer.

As I turned my car back east towards the other side of La Playa, I pondered this case. It wasn't quite as intriguing as I had hoped, but it wasn't as banal as I had feared.

Kim was definitely not the typical mistress. Trey had played with fire when he lied to a biker. I almost pitied him, but not quite.

Then there were the other bikers. I was curious about their club. On the exterior, the leather-clad bikers had fit every stereotype. Tough, manly, a little bit to the left of the law. But they were loyal, that much was clear. Even to Kim, who was new to the club and a woman at that.

And Pin had been so nice. His every move had exuded respect and responsibility. He balanced their books for crying out loud. Although now that I thought about it, balancing the books could still be a bit left to the law. I had seen enough mafia films to know that at least.

But if I was trusting my gut, I would guess he didn't fudge the numbers. I always made sure to listen to my gut, but never let it make the final ruling. Which meant, for now, I was inclined to consider Pin and the other bikers good guys, but I wasn't going to make any major decisions. I had seen plenty of scumbags wearing impressive Good Guy Masks.

If Pin was wearing a mask though, it was a compelling one. My thoughts drifted away from Trey and Kim and towards Pin with the way he had leaned forward to talk to me. The way his eyes had scanned my face as if I was the most fascinating person in the room. The way his hand had brushed against mine when he handed me a beer. The way he had never stared, but had totally and completely noticed my slightly bare midriff. The way one lock of his dark hair had fallen over his forehead.

I shook my head and forced myself to focus on the road. It was not a good idea to mix business with pleasure. I couldn't let a mild crush distract me from the case.

I told myself that my interest in him was because it'd been a while since my last fling. That's why I was so smitten with Pin after a measly two hours. The last guy I'd been with was an artistic type. An aspiring singer-songwriter, which I had thought might make him interesting. Or at the very least poetic.

Veronica had teased me over that one. She had told

endless jokes about how she had been down the aspiring singer road, and it led to nothing but endless complaints and guitars taking up space in one's apartment.

I hadn't even gotten that far. First, he was a mediocre singer. And second, he could converse on exactly one thing, and it was the unfairness of open mic nights in the greater LA area and how it wasn't about talent and all about who you knew.

I'm not saying he was wrong, but after three weeks I was done.

Most of my flings followed that pattern. Different guys, different careers, same impatience on my part. I knew it was more my problem than the guys I dated. I wasn't the type to blame others for my own restlessness.

I also wasn't the type to sit and mope at home. I liked flirting. I enjoyed that fluttery feeling you get in your stomach when you meet a guy who maybe, just maybe, will be different from all the rest. Someone who will make every day an adventure.

Only that guy couldn't be Pin. I would tie up this case with a big bow, wish Kim the best, and then go out and meet someone else. Easy.

By the time I got back to my one-bedroom apartment, it was almost midnight. I sighed but didn't go straight to bed.

Instead, I pulled out my notebook and wrote down all my notes from the night. It was best to record everything while it was still fresh in my mind. I had long since learned that no detail was too small or unimportant. People you thought were side characters could end up being key witnesses.

I wrote down every name of those I had encountered: Moves, Hawk, Carlos, Kim, Trey. Pin. After that, I jotted down physical characteristics and everything they had said, no matter how inconsequential.

Then I turned to a new page and wrote "Outlaw Souls" at the top. I paused with my pen suspended midair. I didn't really know anything about the club, what they did, or how they even made the money that Pin handled.

After a moment of considering how in the dark I was when it came to this biker club, I just wrote a big question mark on the page.

My main priority was sorting out the Trey business and getting Olivia the proof she needed.

But I wasn't going to ignore the Outlaw Souls. They might be a good mystery for a rainy day.

FIVE

PIN

I woke up feeling groggy. It wasn't a hangover. It wasn't even that I hadn't slept well. I got home from Blue Dog Saloon well before midnight, and it was just past eight when I got out of bed. If anything, I hadn't slept so soundly in a long while.

It was something about the night. I had gone in expecting the usual: a few beers with my brothers, small talk about the club, maybe some light tension over whatever our rival club, Las Balas, were up to.

Instead, it had turned into one of the more dramatic nights I had ever lived through. Although, that wasn't strictly true. I had endured plenty of more action-packed evenings (it came with the biker territory).

But for some reason, the evening before had felt monumental.

I tried to shake off my melodramatic musings as I hopped into a scalding shower. Nothing had actually *happened*. Yeah, it turned out Kim's new boyfriend was a prick, and the cute blonde Moves dragged over being a freaking PI was an interesting plot twist, but none of that involved me.

But it involved Claire, I thought. *And maybe she involves me.*

I frowned and stared through the steam at the white tiles in my shower. No way. This was not a good path to go down. She wasn't even interested. She had been pretending for her job. I was just a means to get closer to Kim.

I didn't blame her for that. She clearly was a skilled PI, and I appreciated how she had been upfront with Kim in the end.

But she had still been using me.

Which meant every little smile, each wide-eyed question, every time we had made eye contact, that all meant nothing. Which was fine.

I reminded myself for the umpteenth time that I hadn't been looking to pick up anyone the night before, and if I had, I certainly would not have chosen Claire. She was way too complicated for my tastes.

I stepped out of the shower and grabbed a towel, drying myself down. I needed to stop talking myself in circles. I had other things to think about today. I was due to meet a few of the brothers to go over some numbers and discuss a few jobs we had in the works.

Things had been tense with the Las Balas. We had been staying out of their territory and they were avoiding us, but we all knew the fragile peace could never last. It was like the calm before a storm, when the very air seems to crackle with electric tension, sharp enough to sting.

It was all because Balas guys were the worst of the worst. Every negative stereotype about bikers was because of scum like Las Balas. Drugs, sex trafficking, kidnapping. They had their irons in all the worst fires.

I pulled on my clothes and started to throw everything I would need for the day into my backpack. It's not like a club needed to deal with drugs or create prostitution rings to stay afloat. Outlaw Souls was proof of that. We had steady jobs, sometimes even more than we could handle, working security or doing surveillance.

Plus there was the auto shop a few of the older brothers owned and half the club worked at. Everyone in La Playa knew it was the shop to go to if you wanted quality work from mechanics who wouldn't cheat you. At the end of the day, we probably had more profits than Las Balas. And a lot less blood on our hands.

Even so, there were always guys who wanted the easy way out. Who thought dipping a finger in the cocaine pot was the ticket to a better life. I had plenty of experience with guys like that before I even joined Outlaw Souls.

Half of the guys my mom dated when I was growing up were shady as hell. A few of them even got my mother involved which drove me crazy. Especially when I was a kid and couldn't do anything about it.

And the ones that weren't breaking the law were just plain lazy. They would sit around on our couch, watching TV and expecting my mom, who worked two jobs her whole life, to wait on them hand and foot.

I sighed and banished the unpleasant memories. Things weren't like that anymore. As soon as I graduated from my accounting program, I'd started doing freelance CPA work. Between that and the club, I was able to get my mom her own apartment. I didn't necessarily respect her choices, but I did love her.

I surveyed my clean apartment one last time before heading out. It wasn't much, but it was mine and I had earned it the honest way.

I hopped on my bike and steered it towards the auto shop where the meeting was. After that, I needed to finish up some tax work for a company I was freelancing for.

I frowned beneath my helmet. As the colorful signs blurred by, I felt a twinge of guilt. I hadn't visited my mom in a while. I knew I should try and find time to swing by for dinner, but it would just mean more irritating memories.

Whenever I visited my mom, I felt about fifteen again. Fifteen and frustrated with her and furious at her boyfriends.

Although when I was fifteen, I had handled it all wrong. I had gone out and done the stupidest thing I've ever done: I got a girlfriend.

Her name was Sara Garcia, and she made my teenage heart stop dead in its tracks. She had big brown eyes, always wore those little cut-off jean shorts that high school girls wore, and had the loudest laugh. I think it was her laugh that really made me fall for her. I was so miserable that I was desperate to be around some joy. I wanted just a fraction of Sara's happiness.

And for a while, I had that happiness. I had all the arrogance of youth, walking down the hallways hand-in-hand with Sara and thinking I had it all figured out.

I cringe when I look back at how idiotic I was. I thought every date with Sara was the best date ever. When we went to the movies and I snuck my arm around her, it was the best evening of my life. Until a week later, when we made out for hours on her bed. We did it all together. We went to school dances and I watched her during her cheerleading practices. After a few months of dating, we took each other's virginities.

I thought she was the one. My mom had made mistakes

in love, but not me. I had found someone I could trust. Someone who would never hurt me.

Yeah. I was wrong.

It happened right after our six month anniversary, and yes, it killed me that I kept track of shit like that.

There was a big house party hosted by one of Sara's friends one Friday. I had to work pretty late at my busboy job, but we agreed to meet at the party.

I walked in around eleven, and the first person I ran into was this girl Sara knew. I didn't even know her very well, but I could tell right away something was off. I asked her where Sara was, and if pity had an odor, that girl would have been reeking. I could see in her eyes, in the way she opened her mouth but didn't speak, that wherever Sara was, it was not gonna make me feel good.

I wish I had just walked away, but instead, like the stubborn fool I was, I went looking for Sara. I found her in one of the bedrooms, buck naked with another guy.

For a second, I thought she was drunk and he had taken advantage. I was ready to beat the shit out of him for dragging my wasted girl to that bed.

But then Sara looked up. She was not drunk. She was clear-eyed and clearly enjoying it. When she saw me, she had the decency to stop and pull a bed sheet around her chest. The other guy made a quick exit, but took the time to toss me a little smirk and a "Sorry, man."

Sara said what they always say. She just got carried away. She thought I was such a great guy, but things had happened so fast, and she wasn't perfect.

And I just stood there with my heart breaking in two.

I wasn't mad at her though. I was angry at myself. Because I should have known better. How many times had I seen my mom throw herself into a relationship with a guy who didn't care enough to be loyal?

And I couldn't be mad at Sara. She was just acting on human nature.

So I decided the next day that my heart wasn't broken. Love was a hallucination. Love never lasted, and people were always going to act on their own self-interests. Which meant that something as fake as love wasn't going to stop someone from cheating.

In a way, I was grateful for Sara. I should have learned earlier, but at least I learned. After that, things really did get better. I discovered bikes and the club and my career. I enjoyed plenty of women, but I steered clear from all the long-term nonsense.

And I never got hurt or humiliated again.

But somehow, being around my mom made me forget all that. It made me feel young and stupid again. She'd kept pestering me about why Sara and I broke up, so I ended up telling her what'd happened. My mother had actually patted me on the shoulder and told me that I couldn't give up. The right girl was out there, I just had to keep trying.

I wanted to tell my mom that if trying to find Mr. Right was what she was doing, then I wanted no part of that. But I didn't say that out loud. My mom had been through enough shit. Most of it of her own making, but I never could bring myself to say anything harsh to her.

I pulled up at the auto shop. I knew that a scowl was etched on my face, but it wasn't my fault that I had woken up to annoying thoughts and memories.

It was Claire's fault. Something about her adorable snub little nose made me think of relationships and how rotten most of them turned out to be. I needed to stop thinking about her nose being adorable.

Raul Lopez, our road captain, was loitering inside, but no one else was around.

"Where is everyone?" I asked.

"Ryder and Moves had to split," Raul said. "Bit of trouble on the other side of town."

I raised my brows.

"Las Balas shit," Raul said. "What else?"

"They need back-up?" I asked, grimacing.

"Nah," Raul said. "I think they just wanted to scare one of the guys who was dealing coke in our territory the other night. Nothing major."

I nodded. It looked like the calm before the storm was starting to give way to drops of rain.

"I'm gonna split then," I said. "Got some work to do."

Raul waved goodbye, and I turned back towards my bike. Just before I hopped on, my phone buzzed. I yanked it out, thinking it might be from Moves or Ryder, but it was from Kim.

We've got a plan for Operation: End Trey.

I rolled my eyes at how dramatic Kim could be. I suppose she had the right since Trey was a liar and a cheat. I read the next text:

*I'm meeting him for a date at Figo Wine Bar downtown on Thursday.
I want my girl Claire to have back-up, so you into play her fake date...
so she can blend in while she gets her evidence?*

I stared into space for a moment. Seeing Claire again was a bad idea. Just one evening with her had tempted me to throw away all my rules about keeping myself to casual hook-ups.

Then again, Claire of all people understood that relationships were all shams. I could tell from the way she discussed Trey and other guys like him that she'd seen her fair share of cheating and betrayal. That meant maybe, just maybe, she understood how it was better to keep things casual.

Not that we would be hooking up. It was a fake date.

And Kim was right that back-up was necessary. A guy like Trey was not going to take kindly to being publicly humiliated by two women. Not to mention that I was pretty positive that Kim had some very public and very scathing words in store for him after Claire acquired proper evidence.

I was sure Kim and Claire could hold their own, but it wouldn't hurt to have someone there to make Trey back off. To help everyone achieve a clean exit should things turn ugly.

My mind made up, I lifted my phone to text Kim:

I'm in.

SIX
CLAIRE

I have always believed in punctuality. In my experience, most bad things only happened because of poor timing.

So when it came to running my cases, I was a stickler for doing whatever necessary to avoid bad timing. Which meant that I decided Pin and I needed to get to the restaurant a good half hour before Kim and Trey's reservation. We needed to be settled in an ideal spot by the time the doomed couple entered.

I had also taken no chances with the seating. I called the hostess ahead to explain the situation. The hostess, herself a past victim of a cheat, had been on board. She promised me that I would have a corner table with a great view, while Trey and Kim would be seated smack dab in the center of the wine bar.

It would still be tricky to get my camera out to snap photos, but I had pulled off similar maneuvers. Besides, I would have Pin to help cover me.

Kim had suggested the fake date. I had laughed it off, but Kim had made some good points. I was way less likely to draw attention to myself if I was sitting with someone.

And Trey's reaction was an unknown factor. I had agreed that Kim deserved to let him have it once I got my photos, so I couldn't say no to an extra body to help us out. I have my pride and I had handled many dicey situations, but I wasn't stupid. I accepted help when it was offered.

At six on Thursday, I ran through my plan one last time to make sure I had everything. I was supposed to meet Pin at half past the hour for our reservation. I hoped he was on time. Then again, I doubted punctuality was something bikers valued as much as I did.

I ducked into my bathroom to swipe a final coat of lip gloss on and admire my outfit. I had to give myself credit: my look walked the perfect line between Date Night and Kick a Cheater to the Curb.

It was a dark burgundy dress with thin straps and a v-neck that showed my cleavage to its best advantage. But it wasn't flimsy. The bodice was fitted and the satin skirt flared out around my hips, falling to my knees which allowed for moveability. I had opted for pointed gold shoes with only half-inch heels. I didn't expect that I would need to run or move anywhere fast, but it was always good to err on the safe side. Just in case.

The truth was, tonight was just for the photos. With Kim's help, I'd managed to build an airtight case against Trey. I had gathered text message screenshots, detailed schedules, and even a few emails. But the wife always wanted a picture. A high quality one too. Blurry photos didn't quite do it.

I had explained to Kim that it would be best if she could be a little touchy with Trey. Maybe even get him to kiss her. Kim had agreed. She was a natural, to be honest. She'd been laser-focused on helping me get all the admin stuff in order so she could have a clear shot when she went in for the kill.

After shoving my notebook, camera, phone and pepper spray into my bag, I called a car. Fifteen minutes later, I was perched on a bench just outside the restaurant.

To my surprise, Pin hopped out of a cab at 6:25 on the dot. I almost didn't recognize him. He had exchanged his leather jacket for a neat button-down with his hair arranged in a neat side part.

He cleaned up well, and was even more handsome away from the dim lights of a seedy bar.

I shook my head and greeted him with a smile. "Thanks for helping out."

"No problem," he said.

We stood in awkward silence for a beat. It wasn't a date, but somehow my nerves were jangling a bit, as if it was.

I took a breath and turned to the door. "Let's do this."

The hostess was good on her word. She threw me a wink as she led Pin and me to a corner table. Pin took the seat with his back to the room so I could sit across from him. It was perfect. Pin's broad shoulders would even conceal my camera. I made a mental note to slip the hostess a twenty before we left.

We ordered drinks – water for the both of us. I needed to keep a clear head and Pin evidently thought the same. I glanced at my watch. We still had thirty minutes. I opened my menu and glanced over the options.

"I'm honestly kinda nervous," Pin said.

I looked up to see he was wearing a self-deprecating smile that really had no right to be quite so charming.

"I can't believe you do this kind of stuff every weekend," he said.

"Well, not *every* weekend," I said with a coy shrug.

I ducked my head down to look at my menu. I told myself to stop flirting on the job, but then glanced at my watch again. We had so much time to kill, we might as well enjoy the wait. Besides, Pin wasn't so bad to talk to. There was something about the way he looked at me with total focus. As if I was the only thing in the room worth observing.

"I actually have been getting bored with the cheating husband stuff," I said. "It's not exactly thrilling since these idiots are easy to catch."

"I can imagine," Pin said. "It also must get pretty depressing."

I blinked.

"I guess so," I said. "Honestly, I tend to disassociate. I don't often involve the mistress like tonight; Kim's an exception. And something tells me she doesn't need my pity."

"Don't call Kim a mistress to her face," Pin said with a grin. "She definitely won't like that."

I laughed as I pictured Kim's outraged reaction to being labeled a mistress. "Noted. Thanks for the advice."

Figo Wine Bar was trendy and right in the center of downtown La Playa. Even on a Thursday night, it was filled with couples gripping big glasses of wine and nibbling on tapas. I knew this wasn't a real date, but something about the piano music in the background and the shimmering orbs hanging artfully from the ceiling for lighting made me feel all smiley and chatty, as if it was a first date with a really, really cute guy.

Because Pin was cute. More than cute. He was downright attractive. And I couldn't help but steal a glance at his torso. I could see the shape of his shoulders and chest through the thinner fabric of his shirt and he was definitely fit. I flashed my eyes back to his face.

"So what's next?" he asked. "Now that you've gotten bored with all the cheaters."

"I'd love to bust a criminal ring or something," I said. "Missing children cases can be really rewarding too. I worked one a few years ago with a coworker."

"What happens when you don't solve a case though?" Pin asked.

"Oh, I drink," I said.

That shocked a snort of laughter out of him.

"Yeah," I said. "I do not deal well with failure. I was always a very sore loser as a kid."

"Isn't failure unavoidable?"

"Of course," I said. "And knowing when it's time to close a file is part of the job. Doesn't mean I like it."

"But you love the job anyway," Pin said.

It wasn't a question. He could tell how dedicated I was to my PI work. I held still as I met his gaze and nodded. His perception made a chill run up and down my bare spine.

"What about you?" I asked. "How did you get sucked into the dubious world of biker clubs?"

"Trust me, Outlaw Souls is nothing close to dubious." Pin gave a dry chuckle. Even his laughter was cute. "We're a strictly above-board club. Bikes, security jobs, brotherhood, and that's about it."

"I didn't know there was such a thing as an 'above-board' biker club," I said.

"Well, there is," Pin said. His tone wasn't too sharp, but his face darkened and I could tell I had offended.

"I'm sorry," I said. "I guess I've only been exposed to stereotypes."

"Not your fault," Pin said.

"Well, I don't like being ignorant," I said. "Tell me more about the club."

Pin's smile said he was all too happy to move on. He told me about a few of his brothers and the rides they went on before explaining his accounting work. Then he asked me more questions about how I got into the PI world, and what my favorite cases were.

He laughed out loud when I told him the story about a time I talked my way into a business conference at an exclusive LA hotel by pretending I was on the board of a Norwegian company because I was convinced a guy was meeting his mistress there. I discovered it was an actual work conference and the guy was there for business only.

"Rest assured, I got him a week later," I said. "It just turned out he preferred cheap motels for his trysts."

Pin was easy to talk to. A little bit serious, but he could be funny, in a quiet and slightly sarcastic kind of way. Then again, lots of guys I'd gone out with had been easy to talk with. Didn't mean they weren't boring after the first few dates.

Before I knew it, I caught a glimpse of Kim and Trey settling down at their table.

"Ok, don't turn around," I said to Pin, keeping a casual smile plastered on my face. "But our targets have arrived."

Pin instantly stiffened.

"Please relax," I said. "We're just having a nice evening, ok?"

Pin nodded, and his shoulders eased slightly.

I kept my eyes on Pin, but stole glances over at the table. Kim was decked out in a silver dress with a slit up to her hip and sky-high heels. She looked like a million bucks. I smiled as I sipped my water and grabbed a fry from the plate Pin and I were sharing. She really was trying to torture Trey.

He was smitten too, I could tell. He was ogling Kim with that wide-eyed look of admiration mixed with a healthy dose of pride. I saw it all the time. Guys were so self-congratulatory when they convinced some young hot thing to choose them.

What killed me was that Olivia was no crone. I had seen the pictures. She took good care of herself. Probably had worked out like crazy to shed her baby weight after giving birth. She went to the hairdresser and did her makeup all while dealing with an infant.

But Trey didn't see any of that. Guys like Trey enjoyed the chase. Once they had the woman all secure and in their bedroom, they lost interest. They started to look for something newer, younger, hotter.

"She's doing a great job," I said to Pin. "She's got him wrapped around her finger."

"I would expect nothing less from Kim," he said.

Kim and Trey had ordered, but they were ignoring their glasses of wine. Instead, Kim was leaning forward while Trey ran his hand up and down her smooth brown arm.

"Ok, I'm gonna pull my camera out," I said. "You just keep chatting while I set it up."

"About what?" Pin asked.

"Anything," I said. "Just act normal."

"I did some freelance CPA work today," Pin said. "Really interesting situation with their profit margins."

I nearly laughed out loud as I pulled my camera up onto the table. "You're really talking about accounting?"

"You said I could discuss anything," he said.

"Fair enough," I said. "Please tell me more about profit margins."

Pin gave me a crooked smile and continued. While he talked, I screwed the lens in place and made sure the shutter wouldn't clack with a noise when I took a photo.

Kim was facing me, so I had Trey's profile, but he was

unlikely to see me. I knew I could count on Kim to stay in it until I gave her the signal.

I got a series of photos of him rubbing her arm and then to top it off, he leaned in and kissed her neck.

"Perfection," I muttered. "This is borderline art."

Pin snorted. "I hope the wife agrees."

"Oh, she won't," I said. "But her lawyer will love these."

I set my camera down. I had more than enough. It was time for the signal. I quickly took apart my camera and slipped it back into my bag. "Ok, I'm good."

I leaned to the side so Kim could see me past Pin. Then I lifted my hand up to the chunk of my hair that fell over my collarbone and flicked it over my shoulder with a toss of my head for emphasis.

"A hair flip?" Pin asked. "That's the super secret signal?"

"You should turn around now," I said. "You're gonna wanna see this show."

SEVEN
PIN

I twisted in my chair as soon as Claire gave me the ok. It had been agony keeping myself from sneaking a glance at Kim.

Well, not total agony. Claire was more than a decent diversion. To be frank, she was downright hot when she was in her investigation element. But I still was dying with curiosity to see what was going on with Kim and Trey.

As soon as I turned around, Kim started to raise her voice so that it carried over to us.

"It's so funny that you say that Trey," Kim said. "Because I've heard I'm *not* actually the one for you."

Trey didn't look scared yet, just confused.

"In fact, I've had it on really good authority that you have a wife," Kim said.

A few people in the restaurant gasped aloud. Trey looked terrified.

"Baby, calm down," Trey said. "Who told you that?"

"Oh, do *not* call me baby," Kim said, standing up so she could look down at Trey.

I glanced back at Claire. Her eyes were lit up with

excitement. She looked like a kid on Christmas morning and it was totally cute. She wiggled her eyebrows at me.

"Told ya it would be good," she whispered.

"Look, Trey, I'm not even angry," Kim said. "Because I know you're going to get what's coming to you. I just feel *bad* for you."

By this point, the whole restaurant had fallen silent while Kim's voice only got louder.

"Seriously," Trey hissed through clenched teeth. "Don't even think about going to my wife about this."

"Oh, I wouldn't dream of it," Kim said.

Kim had one hand on her hip with her leg stuck out just so Trey could get the best view of what he was missing. Then, her every movement part of her performance for the crowd, Kim picked up her big glass of fancy red wine.

"Oh shit," I muttered.

"My thoughts precisely," Claire said.

Kim dumped the entire glass of wine onto Trey's crisp white shirt. The restaurant erupted into cheers and the hostess even let out a loud whistle.

"That's our cue to leave," Claire said.

I turned to see that she had already risen to her feet and packed her purse up.

"I gave my card to the hostess ahead of time," Claire said, winking at me. "In my line of work, sometimes you gotta bolt fast."

Now I've engaged in plenty of flirtations. I've seen the batted eyelashes, the hair twirled around a finger, the coy smile, but I had never had a girl wink at me. And for some reason, that half-second movement from Claire made my stomach drop right to the floor.

She was too good to resist.

I stood up and followed her as she whisked Kim away.

All the while Trey was mopping up his shirt, so he never actually saw Claire. It was expertly done.

Once we were out on the sidewalk, we speedwalked until we were a few blocks away. Then Kim let out a big whoop.

"Fuck, that felt good!" she said. "I've always wanted to throw my drink at a guy!"

"You killed it," Claire said. "Looked like you'd done it a million times."

The girls high-fived, and I couldn't help but grin. Kim had been a true showstopper, but my eyes kept lingering on Claire's face and the way her button nose scrunched up when she smiled.

I had rules about never going for the women who made me feel too much. The ones who stirred up blind desire. That was reckless. That kind of desire had led to the mess with Sara.

But if Claire was going to wear that dark red dress and do things like wink sassily at me while she said something badass, I was going to throw every single rule out the window.

"You get what you need?" Kim asked.

"I got more than enough," Claire said. "Thanks again for all your help, this is my new record for tying up a case."

I stiffened. Claire spoke with a tone of finality as she patted her bag. As if she was getting ready to call it a night. Go home. Tie up her case. And I would never see her again.

As if she read my thoughts, Kim grabbed Claire's arm.

"Well then you have *got* to let me buy you a drink," Kim said. "You've got a new record, and I'm newly single, that's worth celebrating."

Claire chewed on her bottom lip as she considered.

"Come *on*," Kim begged. "You have to at least have one

drink out of pity for the poor girl who got duped by an asshole. I never would have figured it out if not for you."

"Ok, just one drink," Claire said with a laugh.

Kim jumped up and down and squealed in excitement. "Ok, let me call a car to take us to Hive. I need to dance."

Claire's eyes widened when Kim mentioned one of the biggest clubs in La Playa, but she didn't turn away.

"You would have figured Trey out," Claire said. "And it wouldn't have taken you very long."

"Probably," Kim said with a shrug.

Kim knew the bouncer at Hive, so we were able to cut the line and buy drinks in no time.

I tried not to stare, but I couldn't help but notice the way Claire's pale face seemed to shimmer beneath the disco lights. And the way she scanned the room with an excited gleam in her eye, as if anything could happen at any moment, and she would be ready to leap into action.

When she reached up to push her hair off the back of her neck, I was tempted to run my finger down her nape, just to feel how smooth her skin was.

After one round, Kim declared it was time to dance. She strutted out towards the dance floor like she owned it. Within minutes, she was dancing with an eager guy.

"Is she always the life of the party?" Claire asked me.

"Dunno," I said, liking the way she leaned in towards me as if we were co-conspirators. "I haven't gone out with her a ton."

"Well, I think she's amazing," Claire said. "And she deserves this after Trey."

Her mouth flattened into a frown when she mentioned Trey. I wanted to make her forget him. I wanted to make her forget every guy that wasn't me.

It occurred to me that she could have a boyfriend. In

fact, it was likely she did. But then, on the off chance she was single, I had to try my luck.

"Wanna dance?" I asked.

"Sure," Claire said. She hopped down from the barstool and followed me towards the floor.

"I should warn you, I'm a terrible dancer," she said.

"Me too," I said.

She was not a terrible dancer. She just didn't dance like other women. First off, she didn't even try to be sexy. There was no sensual wiggling of her hips or gyrating. Instead, Claire just danced however she wanted. She jumped and twirled and spun her arms around and laughed.

Claire wasn't trying to be anything besides who she was. It was the sexiest thing I had ever seen.

I couldn't take my eyes off her small but wiry form. I wanted to trace the indent of her waist with my hand and run my other hand along the curve of her muscled upper arms.

But I didn't. I kept my distance. I grabbed her hand to twirl her and, when she didn't let go, I twirled her again. One song bled into another, and eventually she edged closer and closer to me. I got more and more lost in the way her eyes flashed when she looked up at me. There was something there, I could tell.

Then she was only inches away, and I gripped her back with my hand while we spun. Like it was as easy as breathing, she draped her arms over my shoulders while my other hand found her waist.

We danced like that for a while before having another round of drinks. Kim tracked us down at one point, and we all danced together, but I didn't plan on leaving Claire's side. She seemed ok with that.

It was on the wrong side of midnight when the three of

us exited onto the sidewalk. Kim had danced with a bunch of people and even made out with a guy in the bathroom, but she wasn't going home with anyone. She was not the type of girl who needed to fuck a rando to get over a guy.

"Claire!" Kim squealed. "You're the best, and I love you."

She wrapped her arms around Claire and hugged her. Given that Kim was at least six inches taller than Claire even without her heels, I was concerned that Claire was going to get squished. Kim had definitely taken a tequila shot or two with her dance partners.

"Thanks," Claire said. "You're the best too!"

Claire then helped Kim call a car. Kim waved goodbye to us one last time before departing.

So it was just me and Claire, alone on the sidewalk. The music from inside the club throbbed behind us, but the crowds were a distant memory. The world shrunk to the two of us, beneath a streetlight's glow.

"Fun night," I said.

Claire nodded. She looked at the ground and then glanced up at me from beneath her lashes.

"You want to split a car?" she asked.

She had no clue where I lived, and I didn't know where she lived. For all we knew, we could be on opposite ends of La Playa.

But there was no way in hell I was saying no to her.

"Sure," I said.

Claire asked with my address and then fiddled with her rideshare app for a few seconds. "It'll be here in five minutes."

A bevy of giggling women stumbling out of the club's side door made us move up against the wall. As the women tumbled into cars and disappeared, I stepped closer to Claire.

I hadn't known her long, but I knew that she was fearless and bold. And yet as I lifted my hand to touch her jaw, I moved with agonizing slowness, like she was a scared animal likely to bolt.

Maybe I was the one who was scared.

As my fingers rested just near her ear, she lifted her chin and locked her eyes on mine. At that moment, I knew that she wanted me just as much as I wanted her.

I leaned down, and she raised herself on her tiptoes so that our lips met. I pressed gently at first, but then she did this little gasp. Just a quick intake of breath, but I couldn't hold back.

I deepened the kiss and ran my tongue between her lips. She wrapped her arms around my neck and pressed her entire body against my torso, making it so I was the one gasping with desire. My entire body caught on fire as I gripped her waist with one hand and moved my other hand lower, just above the curve of her ass.

The buzz of her phone made her pull away. I clenched my teeth so I didn't growl out a curse.

Claire blinked as if she was waking from a dazed sleep, then she yanked her phone out of her purse. "The car's here."

EIGHT
CLAIRE

I told myself it did not mean anything that Pin was the best kisser I had ever encountered.

Some guys were good at kissing. So what? It didn't mean that he was different or special than any other hook up. And he was totally a guy to hook up with. That's it.

We slid into the backseat of the car in silence, but the air seemed to crackle between us. Because, Jesus Christ, he was a good kisser.

As a rule, I don't like PDA. I'm the type of girl who keeps her head. But as soon as his lips brushed mine, I forgot everything. I forgot we were on the sidewalk outside of a club, which is such a painfully cliche place to make out. I forgot that he was a biker from the wrong side of town who probably had like five biker chicks on rotation.

I was only consumed with the flames of desire coursing through my blood as he pulled me tighter with a grip that was somehow strong as iron yet gentle.

I looked at him out of the corner of my eye. Our thighs were a good ten inches apart, and yet I was aching with the desire to throw myself into his lap.

When he caught me looking at him, I quickly turned my head toward my phone. We were about five minutes from my place. I had put in his address as well. This whole night could end in five minutes. I didn't have to be thrown for a loop by his spellbinding kisses. But then, I wouldn't get to kiss him again. And I really wanted to kiss him.

I scoffed at my longing. I didn't even know him. A laugh escaped my mouth.

"What?" Pin asked.

I shook my head and turned to him with wide eyes. "I just realized I don't even know your real name."

"Pin is a real name," he said.

I clapped my mouth shut. I forgot how serious he took his biker club. I shouldn't have disrespected his biker name.

I breathed a sigh of relief as he flashed me a kind smile.

"But my other name is Gabriel," he said. "Gabriel Gallegos."

"Gabriel," I repeated. It suited him in a way. It was old fashioned and solid. Masculine but with a touch of class.

"I like it," I said. "But I think I like Pin better."

His face erupted in a smile so genuine that my heart started beating twice as fast. When had I become so soft and girly? When had I started obsessing over the way a man *smiled*?

I had friends who were like this. Who would describe the play by play of meeting a guy as if it was an epic saga? I always hid my eye-rolls. Because could one guy *really* be all that interesting? Could he be more thrilling than backpacking across Europe? Or living in a van in Alaska for a year? Or going undercover as a spy? Or one of the other thousand things I wanted to try in my life?

No. One guy could not be all that. He could not be my be-all, end-all.

It just so happened that maybe Pin was all that for this one night. Maybe. I glanced at him again. His knee was jiggling up and down in a restless motion.

I reached out and placed my hand atop his thigh. It was the first touch since our kiss had ended. He froze. When he looked at me, I lost my breath due to the intensity in his eyes.

The car pulled to a stop.

"This is me," I said. "Do you wanna come up?"

His nod was quick and resolute. In times of uncertainty, I acted on instinct. It's what made me a good PI. My instincts had gotten me out of tight spots more times than I could count.

It felt good to let go and just trust my gut.

I was almost shy as I led the way into my apartment. Most of the guys I hooked up with were business types from La Playa. I had never so much as chatted with a biker. His world had to be so different from mine.

He looked at my decor with interest. I mostly had maps. World maps, city maps. A schematic of the greater LA area. A California road map. I liked to think about how big the world was. But wall art didn't hold his attention for long.

I stood in the middle of the room and looked up at him. He was three feet away, but somehow I felt his eyes assessing me. For once, I was at a loss for what to say. I usually had a quippy comment or a joke, but when faced with Pin, I drew a complete blank.

I didn't need to speak though. He closed the distance between us in one stride, and we were kissing with a fervor. I pressed myself against his firm chest and tipped my neck back to give him easy access to my lips, but the contact wasn't enough. I wanted more.

As if he read my thoughts, Pin placed one hand under my bottom and pulled me up. I wrapped my legs around his waist. The skirt of my dress slid up my thighs in a satisfying rush of silk. I grinned when I realized that his kisses were even better when our faces were at the same level.

He moved his lips away from my mouth and to my neck. I gasped in excitement as he expertly tickled the skin just below my ear. I wasn't shy anymore. I wanted one thing: him.

His palms burned an imprint on my back, and yet I craved more. I wanted to feel his hands all over me. I captured his lips again and tried to pour all my yearning into my kiss. He let out a small groan of desire that thrilled me to my core, and then took a step forward.

He was stronger than I had realized. He wasn't overly muscled, but he had a wiry form, as if he was all leather and iron instead of skin and bone.

"Bed?" he muttered. "Where is it?"

I pulled away, catching my breath.

"Through that door," I said with a nod in the right direction.

In three long strides, he was kicking open my door, stepping into the darkness of my bedroom.

"Careful," I giggled. "Don't drop me."

"I would never." His words were mumbled, deep and sensual, into the hollow of my collarbone.

I squirmed with pleasure at just the sound of his voice. I had it bad for him, that was certain. I released his hips from my legs and hopped out of his arms.

He made a little humph of displeasure, but I wanted the lights on for this. I flicked the lamp beside my bed on and turned to look at him, illuminated in the soft glow. My breath hitched as I took in his hooded eyes, dazed with masculine desire. All for me.

I locked my eyes with his and didn't blink as I slipped the straps of my dress off my shoulders, letting it tumble to the floor in a burgundy heap. I kicked off my shoes and stepped toward him, clad in only my black bra and underwear.

His eyes roved over my body, savoring every single inch as I closed the distance. I shivered with anticipation as he grinned when I started unbuttoning his shirt. He reached down to the buckle of his pants, but I swatted his hands away. I wanted to undress him myself.

I thought he might be confused, but his smile only widened. His chest was the same tanned brown as his face, but it had a soft thatch of dark hair. I skimmed my fingers down over his hard stomach and slipped them beneath the waistband of his jeans.

Then his hands were on me. One gripped my bare back, and the other placed on my ribcage, just below the hem of my bra. I kissed him again while I undid his belt buckle.

He let out something like a growl as his pants fell to the floor and then pushed me back towards the bed. I smiled. He wanted to take control. I could work with that. Something told me that he was going to be very good at this.

We tumbled onto the bed, and he rolled onto his back. In an instant, I was straddling him. His hands fell to my hips as if they belonged there.

I sat still and just looked down at him, taking him in. His skin seemed to glow with need, and his hair had long since fallen out of the neat side-part. He lifted his hips and shifted me, my mouth opening in delight as I felt the evidence of his want. He was so hard for me.

I leaned down and kissed him again. As I did, he started to pull my underwear down. I was about to ask him exactly how he planned to get them off of me while I was atop him, but before I could speak, he flipped me over onto my back, now on to. Without even thinking, I raised my hips so he could dispose of the underwear.

His lips skimmed over my skin. My neck, my shoulder, the hollow of my clavicle. He nudged at my bra and I suddenly grew desperate with impatience. I pushed him up just slightly and unclasped my bra, casting it to the side as quickly as I could.

I gripped his torso to pull him back onto me, arching my back with a sigh as his mouth found my right nipple. He licked and sucked with eagerness, even as his fingers expertly fondled my other breast.

I slid my hands down his back, enjoying the feel of his firm muscles, until I reached his boxer shorts. I yanked at the elastic and pushed my hand underneath the waistband. I wanted to feel how hard he was.

He let out a groan against my breast as I slid my hand up and down his solid length. He wanted me badly, and my pussy throbbed with longing, already sopping wet for him. I pushed my hips up against his, encouraging him to take me then and there. Instead, he moved down, skimming his lips over my stomach until he reached my satin folds.

His tongue flicked my clit, and even as I whimpered in pleasure, I didn't want him to feel obligated.

"Pin, you don't have to," I gasped.

"Be quiet," he said. "I've been thinking of doing this all night."

Flames erupted deep inside me at his words, and I lost all ability to speak as he sucked and licked with mounting intensity. Wave after wave of ecstasy washed over me until I was gasping for breath. I moaned and even begged. I would have been ashamed at how much I screamed for satisfaction, but I couldn't think of anything but Pin and the way he was kissing and touching me.

I felt myself rising to a climax and I wove my fingers through his thick hair. His hands tightened on my thighs, as if he was determined to keep me close to him even as I bucked in physical delight.

"Oh God." I moaned. "I'm so close."

When I orgasmed, I saw stars. Pleasure coursed through my body as I rode the sensations higher and higher, lost in the sexual ecstasy.

That's what I had wanted, all night as I had danced with Pin. I didn't want to think about how he might bore me in a week, or consider how wise it was to hook up with a biker. I just wanted to chase the feeling of intimacy and sexual pleasure.

As I came back down, I slid my hands to his shoulders, trying to encourage him to move. He had given me so much, but I knew I wanted more. I wanted to give him what he had given me.

He rose up above me, a soft smile on his face. It wasn't an arrogant grin, I could tell. He didn't want a pat on the back over going down on me. He genuinely was pleased to see me so satisfied.

I pushed on his chest and sat up. He furrowed his brow in confusion, but rolled onto his back. I reached over and fumbled in my bedside drawer until I had pulled out a condom. He grabbed it from me and tore at the wrapper.

When he was ready, I straddled him again and sucked in my breath at the feel of his hard cock against my thigh. I whispered, "Is this ok?"

"Yes," Pin said, eyes steady.

I smiled and slowly lowered myself onto him. He closed his eyes as I took him inside me, embedding him up to his hilt. He moaned as I rose up and down again, and I grinned at how much pleasure I was clearly giving him.

"Oh God, you feel so good," he gasped.

I let out a sigh of victory as I positioned myself so he reached a spot deep inside me.

And then I let myself go.

I rode him hard as he bucked his hips to keep up with me. I kept riding him as he moaned. His hands ran up my hips to knead my breasts and then back down over my stomach.

When his panting reached a desperate level, I felt myself instinctively clenching around him, urging him onto his own climax. He cried out as he was pushed over the edge. I watched him spasm with pleasure and rode his orgasm out.

When he had finished, I leaned down while he was still inside me and placed a gentle kiss on his mouth. Then I rolled off him and onto my beck. We lay in silence, a warm cloud of satisfaction enclosing us both.

I moved to my side, facing him and reveling in the warmth of his large body. He shifted closer to me and raised his arm. I didn't usually cuddle, but his chest looked so enticing that I rested my head against him. I sighed as he wrapped his arm around my waist.

The exhaustion of the day caught up to me. Every second of the night, from Trey's downfall to the dancing to the sex had been absolutely thrilling, but my energy had been expended.

I knew that maybe we should talk. I knew how to define hook-ups, I had plenty of practice. I needed to set boundaries. I needed to say something about how fun it was, so it would be clear that "fun" was all I was looking for.

But before I could speak, my eyelids drooped, and I fell into darkness.

NINE
PIN

I dozed for a little bit, the soft weight of Claire's body a warmth that somehow captured my entire form, but a gut instinct woke me up in the small hours of the morning.

Some part of me knew it wasn't healthy to linger. It encouraged clinginess and feelings. Sex was one thing, but actually sleeping together until the sun rose was another beast. You could fall asleep thinking one thing, and then wake up thinking quite another.

The sex had been amazing. Every second had been so fucking hot that I had almost thought it was a dream. But Claire's gasps and moans and delightful little hands had convinced me it was all real. I had felt my soul shatter as Claire moved above me.

I didn't want to admit it, but if I really looked back at my exploits, it would have been no contest. It was the best sex of my life.

But sex was just sex.

I needed to get out of there before it moved into something else. Something dangerous. As I lay there in the dark, Claire's soft breathing tickling my ear, I refused to think about Sara and high school and my mom. I wouldn't go there. I couldn't.

As gently as I could, I shifted her away from me and onto the pillows. She didn't even stir. I smiled to myself. It was no surprise she was a deep sleeper. When she was awake, she was so alive and buzzing with energy, it made sense that when she slept, it would be absolute.

Even so, I was careful to make as little noise as possible as I fumbled in my discarded pants for my phone while using the flashlight to locate the rest of my clothes. I did my best to not glance at Claire's lacy black bra on the floor, but I wasn't that strong.

My stomach lurched as I realized that I wanted to see her in that bra again. I wanted to take it off her. Again and again. That was why she was dangerous. That kind of deeper intimacy and emotion could only lead to pain.

I exited her room, finished getting dressed and headed for the door.

I didn't look back.

The sun was peeking over the horizon when I finally made it back to my place. I had thought I might get a little more sleep, but I couldn't settle down. I took a shower, changed my clothes, flipped through some accounting tasks.

Nothing held my attention.

Every time I blinked, images of Claire were seared on the inside of my eyelids. Claire perfect pink lips twisting into a smile as I held her. The curve of her pale shoulder. Her flushed face as she came down from the heights of her climax.

Even worse, I kept having nonsexual images too. Claire narrowing her eyes as she pulled out her camera to snapshots of Trey. Claire nodding in appreciation as Kim went in for the kill. Claire's joyous and totally unselfconscious dancing.

A life with Claire would be fun. It would never be dull.

With Claire, it would be something indeed.

But no. I couldn't think like that. That was just like my mother had been. She would have one good date with a halfway handsome guy, and all of a sudden, her head would be filled with daydreams. She would build him into this amazing person and picture this ideal life filled with perfect happiness for years to come.

But even when the guy would prove that he was no good, when it was clear that the years of happiness were going to be years of misery instead, my mother would still cling to her fantasies.

Not me. I didn't make fantasies. I had not glorified anyone since Sara Garcia. She hadn't been worthy of any pedestal, and neither was Claire.

Something within me flinched at putting Claire in the same sentence as Sara.

I groaned and collapsed on my couch. I flipped through the TV channels without aim for awhile, but nothing held my interest. I kept glancing at my phone where it sat on the table next to my couch. When would Claire wake up? Nine? Ten? Or did she sleep past noon after a night out?

When she woke up, would she wonder where I was? She had my number since we had texted to plan out the fake date. Would she text me? Or would she shrug (it was just a casual hook-up after all) and slip into the shower. I felt a tightening of desire when I pictured her in the shower. I had to squash that urge.

Once the morning had faded into afternoon, I knew I had to get out of my apartment. I didn't want to text any of my brothers in case they sensed my mental unrest and decided to get all nosy. I just wanted a bit of a distraction. Something to get my mind off Claire.

So I pulled out my drive and pointed my bike towards the auto shop. There had to be someone hanging out. And willing to talk about something other than women.

It occurred to me as I approached the back of the shop that Kim might be around. I knew she was no idiot. Everything had been a little blurry thanks to the alcohol, but I could have sworn Kim gave me a knowing look as she hopped into her car.

There were already too many people in my life that liked to play matchmaker, so I would not put it past Kim. For all I knew, Kim might have been orchestrating the whole night so that Claire and I ended up together at the end. I wondered if Claire had been in on it. Had she told Kim she wanted to be alone with me? Had Kim helped her achieve that goal?

Even more relevant, had Claire communicated with Kim after the fact? Girls did that. They got in touch as soon as the date or hook-up was over to dissect every little thing.

My mood darkened. Had the sex been good for Claire? Would she give Kim a favorable report? She must be texting someone because she certainly wasn't texting me.

I cursed under my breath and reminded myself that I didn't want her to text me or reach out at all. That was why I had left so early.

I cast furtive eyes around the shop as soon as I entered. No sign of Kim. I breathed a sigh of relief.

"Pin, what up man?"

I turned and smiled at Moves as he strode out of the office. We clasped hands in greeting.

"Nothing much," I said.

I followed Moves into the backroom where we both

lolled on the ragged armchairs that had been dragged back there. He gestured to a small fridge. "You want a beer?"

"Nah, I'm good." If I started drinking now, I could end up drunk by nightfall. While sober me was totally in control, I didn't want to think about if my drunk alter ego could avoid sending Claire a message.

"Well, I'm gonna indulge," Moves said, opening the fridge. "I need one after all the Las Balas bullshit."

I raised my brows as I remembered. This was good. Or, well, not good, but it was a real issue. Something actually important. "What went down the other day?"

"We just got word of some dealing on our territory," Moves said, taking out a beer. He opened it and frowned, eyes zoned out as he seemed to think. "It wasn't a big deal, but something was off."

"What do you mean by off?" I asked.

Moves had been around the block. He didn't get rattled by just anything, nor did he overthink. He was the enforcer. If something was out of line, he cracked some heads, told a joke, and moved on.

"We ran the dealer down outside some seedy bar," Moves said. "I hadn't even seen this guy before."

"So?" Not even Moves had a catalog of every active dealer in La Playa. They came and went so quickly, popping up, getting sent off to a stint in jail, coming out of jail, moving towns, or straight-up just dying (and not of natural causes).

"Dunno," Moves said. "Just something off about him."

I didn't want to badger Moves, but he was going to have to be more specific before I got concerned. I was the analytical one in the club. I trusted facts and hard data. I didn't make decisions off of bad vibes. Not to say that Moves made bad decisions. He had excellent instincts. It just wasn't my way.

"Young," Moves said. "He was real young."

I raised my eyebrows and looked at Moves. His face was almost haunted.

"What did you do to him?" I asked.

"Nothing major," Moves said. "Just scared him off, told him to stay outta Outlaw Souls territory."

"How young?" I asked.

"Couldn't say," Moves said. "He'd been using, you know how that fucks you up and makes you look way older."

I nodded. I had come across too many addicts in their twenties who could have easily passed for over forty.

"But something about him," Moves said. "Really young."

Moves glanced at me and his face broke into a wry grin as he shrugged.

"But forget that," Moves said. "Tell me about your night, I hear you went for revenge with Kimmy."

"Yeah, it was pretty funny," I said.

I told him about Kim getting even with Trey, but I was careful to not mention Claire. Just a night with a minor adventure. I could tell that Moves wasn't thinking of her, which meant that Kim, if she was playing matchmaker, had not enlisted Moves' help. Which was all for the best.

Because I was pretty sure I wasn't going to see Claire Brennan ever again.

TEN
CLAIRE

When I woke up, I wasn't certain where I was for a few seconds. When I realized I was in my bed, I was confused. Something was different about my bed.

I rolled over, and there was no Pin where I had fully expected a Pin.

I sat up and checked my clock. It was just after eight. When had he left? I could have sworn he was there when I fell asleep. I had drifted off in his arms with my head rested on his chest. I reached up and touched my hand against my cheek, and then was instantly mortified at the sappy gesture.

It was good that he left. Definitely for the best. If he was still here, I would have to feign politeness and maybe even have coffee with him. All the while I'd be trying to figure out how to let him know it was just casual sex. There was no need for us to waste time with the pleasantries.

Not that it had been bad. Definitely not bad.

Very good, in fact.

But still casual. Still nothing to get serious about.

I rolled out of bed and scampered to the bathroom. I

wasn't that hungover since I hadn't had that much to drink the night before. I just felt hungover for non-alcoholic reasons. My body was worn and tired, my mind blurred with memories from the night before. I could still almost hear the heavy breathing and the moans of pleasure. Nothing a scalding hot shower couldn't banish.

I still had work to do, after all. I needed to compile all the damning evidence against Trey and hand it to Daniel today. Then I would get another case. A better case. There was a small twinge of regret when I pictured closing this case. I had been enjoying this particular job. Or at least one part of this particular job.

After the shower, I tugged on my usual outfit for a day at the office; loose jeans and a comfortable T-shirt with some ballet flats. I clipped a chunk of my hair out of my face and fixed myself a breakfast consisting of a muffin and some coffee.

As I chewed my muffin, I decided that I had zero regrets. The night before had been a fun spur-of-the-moment dalliance, but it was a one-time thing. I didn't want to waste any time seeing Pin only to realize that he, like every other guy, was boring and predictable. Underneath the biker leather and the cute smile, could he really be that different?

I needed to focus on my job. If I wanted Daniel to give me better cases, I needed to bring my A-game and advocate for myself. I didn't want to be stuck trailing dumb corporate cheaters for the rest of my days.

If a juicier case came into the firm, and Daniel was busy with something else, he would usually hand it off to Veronica. It made sense. She was my senior and had way more experience than I did. But if I kept finishing up my cheating husband cases as quickly as I could, at some point, Daniel would have to give me a bigger case. Veronica would be tied up, and he would pass the ball to me.

And I would be ready when that time came.

I had to be ready, because I was pretty sure parts of my brain were withering away with every idiot husband I had to track down. I wanted something complex. I wanted twisted motives and dead ends. I wanted the whole bulletin board with a series of photos and notes.

That's why people get into my line of work in the first place. Ask any private investigator, or even a homicide detective, it's not a totally altruistic career. There's this thrill you get when you're chasing something truly elusive. It's almost like an adrenaline high where you can't think of anything else. The mystery of the case consumes you.

I got it a few years back when I tag-teamed an old murder case with Veronica. The guy had died a few years ago so the police had put it aside, but the family was desperate for closure. And unlike the police, private investigators don't have to play by the rules. When Veronica and I caught the scent of the killer, it was amazing. It was the feeling I'd been chasing my whole life.

Yeah, you're also doing it for the people who have been hurt or are missing it. For justice. But when it comes to the thrill of the hunt, you're being selfish. Pin had been incredible, I wouldn't deny that. But when it came to long-term satisfaction, there was no way he could compete with a big case. I wasn't going to let him distract me.

Thirty minutes later, I walked into the office with a spring in my step. I had beaten Veronica and Daniel in, which was fine by me. I sat down at my desk and started putting together everything Olivia Cook would need to get rid of Trey.

An hour later, I was done. I had all the messages

between Trey and Kim, all the photos, plus my own notes and observations. Veronica had arrived by that point and flashed me a smile when I pushed away from my desk with a sigh.

"All done?" she asked.

"Trey Cook is officially screwed," I said.

"Unless the wife gets all sentimental," Veronica said.

It happened sometimes. A wife would see all the evidence, her heart would break, but she wouldn't leave him. He would make some empty promises (probably to get out of paying alimony) and she would choose to believe them. She would close her eyes and tell herself that it wouldn't happen again. He had changed.

It's not fun, but it's not really my problem. I can't tell people how to live their lives.

I glanced down at the photo of Olivia atop my file, and I prayed she had a backbone. Then I waltzed into Daniel's office and tossed the notes onto his desk with a satisfying thunk.

"Finished this already?" he asked.

"Yup," I said.

Daniel leaned back in his chair and regarded me with a wary expression. "Careful, Brennan. A cocky PI makes mistakes."

"I'm not cocky," I said with a saucy grin. "I'm just fast."

He chuckled and leafed through the notes. I knew he wouldn't find anything fishy. There were no cut corners, no sloppy work. I had crossed my t's and dotted my i's.

Daniel tapped his finger on a page of my typed notes. "The mistress Kimberly Delasante. She's the one that's tied to the biker club."

"Yeah," I said. I had kept Daniel appraised of my plan

with the case, including my alliance with Kim. "The Outlaw Souls."

"And you were friendly with her?" he asked.

"I guess," I said. "She came through last night anyway."

So did Pin, but I wasn't about to mention that to Daniel.

"Excellent work, Brennan," Daniel said, flipping through the rest of my notes and then setting the file aside. "As always."

"Thank you," I said. "But you know I want something bigger."

I liked Daniel, and I respected him. I didn't talk back, but I had let him know of my frustration with the easy cases and the cheating husbands. He had assured me that when a case was the right fit, he would make sure I got it. He gave me a big smile, and my heart started racing with anticipation.

"Today is your lucky day," he said. "Sit down."

I sat down in the seat across from him and pulled it closer to his desk. He tapped his hands against the desk, giving me a look. "We haven't officially gotten this case yet, but I met with potential clients yesterday."

"What is it?" I asked. My mind raced with potential issues I could sink my teeth into.

"Two sets of parents with runaway teens," Daniel said. "A fifteen-year-old and a sixteen-year-old, both from La Playa."

"So?" I asked. "Teens run away."

"Yes, that's what the police have told the parents," Daniel said. "But the parents are convinced the teens were coerced by some sort of drug dealing ring."

I raised my brows. That was interesting. "What are the parents like? Social status? Any step-parents or divorce?"

Daniel smiled at my eagerness. He could tell I was chomping at the bit for information.

"Suburban, no divorce," he said. "Seemed like nice people. Classy. White picket fence."

I let out a low whistle. Now that was interesting. Teens run away from poverty-stricken homes or broken families all the time. Most times, if the parents are divorced, the teen runs away from one parent to be with the other one.

But a suburban upper middle-class family had much lower rates of runaways. That wasn't to say that some dark shit can't lurk behind a nice picket fence. The statistics are just different.

"Why do they suspect drugs?" I asked.

"The teens didn't really know each other, but they went to the same school," Daniel said. "West La Playa High – and both of them had been getting mixed up with an older, shadier crowd right before they ran away."

I furrowed my brow. I was already desperate for more details. I needed the age and personality traits of these teens so I could figure out who they were. What would have motivated them to run away from their safe homes? And how would we get them back?

"Brennan, they were mixed up with bikers," Daniel said. "The parents are convinced the biker club is using their kids for drug dealing."

My eyes nearly popped out of my head. "Outlaw Souls."

"The police poked around, but they didn't find much," Daniel said. "But Outlaw Souls is one of the major clubs in the area and let's face it, guys like that are good at evading police questions."

I propped my forearms on Daniel's desk and chewed my lower lip as I thought. Pin wasn't like that. At least I didn't think he was. But it was a big club. What were his so-called brothers like? I had to find out, and I could find out. I just needed to text Pin. Or even Kim. Go out with them at the Blue Dog Saloon again. Keep my eyes open.

"I want this case," I whispered.

"I know," Daniel said. "The parents are considering another PI, but I think they liked me. I made sure to play up your new connection to the Outlaw Souls."

"When will we know for sure?" I asked.

"They should get back to me this afternoon," Daniel said. "As soon as they hire us, it's all yours."

I gave Daniel a massive smile. This was exactly what I wanted. A serious case with different factors. Not just some mopy asshole wanting to feel like a real man with some shiny mistress.

"Thanks," I said. "I won't let you down."

I stood up and headed for the door. The parents would hire us, I was sure of it. I would start researching drug activity in La Playa right away. Once I had all the information and profiles on the teens – the real work would begin.

Then I would figure out how to infiltrate the Outlaw Souls.

ELEVEN

PIN

I never really thought of myself as a fickle guy. Once I made up my mind about something, I stuck to it. I made my choices, and I never looked back or felt regret. I prided myself on sticking to my guns.

I wasn't proud anymore.

Three days after hooking up with Claire, and I was doubting every choice I had made. I had sworn I wouldn't reach out, but I kept talking myself in circles. Maybe she wasn't as risky as I thought. Maybe we could keep it casual as long as we were really clear with each other.

I had gotten a taste with Claire and the day after I convinced myself that just a taste was enough. Now I wanted more. A lot more.

I had my rules and I had stuck to them for a long time, but I was no masochist. I wasn't going to suffer forever. Surely one (or several) more nights with Claire couldn't be dangerous. I would be on guard. I would be careful to keep it casual.

The only question was how to reach out. I had heard nothing from her, but that made sense. I was the one who had booked it out of her apartment. She probably thought I wasn't into it. Which was so deeply untrue, it almost made me angry to think of Claire sitting somewhere imagining that I was ambivalent about our night of passion.

Not that Claire was moping. I hadn't known her long, but I could tell she was not someone to suffer from low self-esteem. She probably had shrugged me off and decided to move on if I wasn't interested. So it looked like I was going to have to make the next move.

As I took care of some accounting business in my apartment, I wracked my head about how to instigate another carnal meeting. The problem was, too much time had passed. If I had texted Claire the day after about how I had a good time, it wouldn't be so out of the blue for me to text her today asking if she wanted to hang. Also, I had no clue how she had reacted to the night. She could be offended by a booty call. Or disinterested.

I shoved my work away and stalked across my apartment in frustrated strides. This wasn't me. I didn't overthink when it came to women. I never hemmed and hawed over how to phrase a text message. If I wanted to hang out with a woman, I usually just asked. If she said no, so what? There were other women for what I wanted.

I paused in my pacing and frowned. Why wasn't that logic working anymore? There were still plenty of other women in La Playa.

But now the idea of simply reaching out to another past hook-up to see if she was game, or going out to a bar to try and meet someone new had no appeal. In fact, I downright winced at the thought of pursuing anyone but Claire.

She had gotten under my skin, that was all. We had chemistry. She was like a scratch I needed to itch. Once I was done, I would go back to other women. It wasn't like I was addicted to her or anything. No one could fall that hard in just one night, especially not me.

I nodded. It was stupid to torture myself any longer by analyzing it. It was time to take action. Since a sudden text seemed too abrupt, I decided I needed a plan with a bit more subtlety.

I checked my watch. I was due to meet a few club members across town for a ride that afternoon. Kim was going to be there. All I had to do was ask Kim if she had heard anything from Claire. It was a normal question to ask. I had helped them out the other night. Kim might even volunteer information.

And if she hadn't heard from Claire, I would suggest we all go out again. Kim could take the lead with organizing it. If all else fails, I would just tell Kim I was interested in Claire. Kim was cool, she wouldn't tease. She had probably already guessed we hooked up, it wasn't like we were being secretive.

Kim could probably sort the whole thing out for me. She could be a little nosy with Claire, find out where she stood, and then let Claire know what I wanted. Girls were good at that kind of thing.

Yeah, it was lazy and felt extremely high school to just let Kim play matchmaker, but I didn't really care. All I cared about was repeating the other night.

I pulled on my jacket and made for the door, a new spring in my step. This was good. I was going to get in touch with Claire, enjoy a few more wild nights until I was satisfied. I would get her out of my system and then move on with my life.

The group was planning on just a quick ride around part of our territory to see how things were. Since the minor incident with the Las Balas dealer the other night, we were all on guard. It was unlikely we would spot anything during daylight hours, but it was good to make our presence known in case Las Balas was planning anything.

We met up at a gas station in Southern La Playa, just off the highway. I smiled as I pulled up and saw the dark curtain of Kim's hair. She was chatting with Hawk. I walked over, nodding a greeting to Hawk.

"Hey, Pin." Kim flashed me a cunning grin, and I could tell she knew or had assumed everything that had happened after we had parted ways outside the club.

"Hey," I said. "How are ya after the other night?"

"Better than ever," Kim said. "But I think Claire was the one who got lucky that night, right?"

She pursed her lips and raised her eyebrows. I chuckled and gave her a casual shrug.

"Are you just guessing or have you talked to Claire?" I didn't want to beat around the bush. We were due to take off on the ride any minute.

"Claire did text me thanking me again, but I wasn't going to pester her about you," Kim said. "But I mean, I have eyes."

Kim was using her eyes to study me up and down. "Did you *want* me to pester her about you?"

I studied the pavement of the parking lot and willed my voice to stay calm. Like it was no big deal. I didn't care either way.

"She's cool, I'd be down to hang out again," I said. "I thought maybe you two had plans or something."

Kim was silent for a moment, her smooth brown face utterly still. Then her eyes widened so much I thought they were going to fall off her brow. "Oh my god. You are so smitten."

"Ok, come on," I said. "Don't be such a girl."

I turned away as if to head back to my bike. I knew it was a low blow to call Kim out on her gender; we were friends in the first place because I didn't nag her about being a girl. But I didn't like the way she was bubbling over with excitement. As if the thing between me and Claire was way more than just sex.

"Fuck off, Pin," Kim said.

She wasn't angry though. Kim was too excited to be angry, and her hands were clasped in front of her chest. "Claire is, like, the coolest. You should totally go for it. She's way better than the bimbos you usually hook up with."

I shrugged off the insult to my history of bimbos since Kim wasn't wrong. Who cared if someone had brains if I was only fucking them for a few nights?

"I dunno," I said. "We haven't talked since the other night."

"Ok, some advice," Kim said. I rolled my eyes but nodded to indicate she should continue. "Claire is a straight shooter, she's not gonna play games with you. So don't fuck around, Pin. Ask her out."

I was saved from answering by Raul hollering that it was time to ride. I was glad of it. I didn't want to tell Kim that I had no intention of asking Claire out on a real date. Now that she had gotten rid of Trey, I didn't want her to give me an "All Men Are Trash and Claire Deserved Better" speech.

If Claire wanted something better, I knew she was more than capable of telling me. I would respect her wishes. I would make it clear that I could only commit to something casual. If she was down for that, then we were great.

As I pushed down on my bike pedal and the engine roared to life, I avoided thinking about what I would do if Claire wanted something more than casual. If she wanted to do the whole relationship thing. If she asked for commitment.

I let the world blur by as my bike picked up speed, and I focused on the feeling of riding in a pack. I belonged here. I knew who I was when I rode with the Outlaw Souls. And I was a guy who couldn't commit to Claire. I would never fully trust any relationship. It wouldn't be a safe haven for me; it would be an Achilles Heel.

I was willing to bet that Claire didn't want a relationship either. Or, if she did, she wasn't the type to move too fast. She would be willing to keep things trivial to start. As soon as I sensed her getting too clingy, I could slam the brakes.

That still didn't solve the issue of how I could reach out. If I buttered Kim up and promised I would be Mr. Good Guy, she would probably be willing to arrange another night out. But I didn't relish the idea of using Kim as a middleman. She was way too much of a meddler.

After we had gone all the way over the section of the territory and found nothing too out of the ordinary, we pulled into another gas station lot to discuss moves. Raul and Hawk wanted to go grab some food, and I was about to agree when I pulled my phone out. And saw a text.

From Claire.

I grinned and opened it up.

Hey Pin! I had fun the other night.
Was wondering if you wanted to hang again tonight?

I resisted pumping my fist in the air. It was my lucky day. And it was just like Claire to not be awkward or beat around the bush with stilted conversation or vague questions. She wasn't asking for a date either, I noted. If she wanted to go out, she would have said that. She wanted to "hang." That was for sure my speed.

I pulled off my riding gloves with my teeth so I could type my response:

I'd be down, I've had a busy few days, does take-out and TV sound good to you?

I told the guys I had to head home to take care of some things and leapt back on my bike. I purposely avoided eye contact with Kim. I was scared she would read something in my face. Now that I didn't need Kim to communicate with Claire, I didn't really want her big nose in my business.

By the time I had made it home, Claire had texted back:

Sounds perfect! Wanna come to mine around 7?

TWELVE
CLAIRE

Daniel had not been kidding. It was a giant case.

The parents had chosen our firm and I had officially been assigned the case only two days ago, but I already had a dozen pages of notes in my leather-bound notebook. I liked to keep all the information in one place and write it down by hand.

It helped me parse through the details and figure out how everything connected. Veronica said I had aggressively neat architect handwriting, with each letter defined like the way engineers write on their diagrams.

I checked my watch. I had an hour before Pin was supposed to arrive. I took a breath and read through all the information I had gathered. I needed to let it soak in, so I could be on high alert for anything Pin said about Outlaw Souls. But I also couldn't overstudy. I had to act natural around Pin and not ask strange questions. Not until he trusted me more, anyway.

The runaway teens in question were named Zoe Hammond and Hector Elenes. The Hammonds and Elenes hadn't been friends, but when both their children packed bags and fled in the night within a month, the parents had found each other. Their stories had shocking similarities.

A few months before running away, Zoe had started dating a new guy. Someone older, according to her friends. The Hammonds had no idea. They only knew that their sixteen-year-old daughter was growing secretive and coming home late and telling lies about where she had been. They were concerned, but figured she was just going through a bit of a rebellious phase.

Mrs. Hammond had teared up when I met with her. She blamed herself. She should have noticed something was wrong with her daughter. Her husband had displayed more anger. Like he wanted to get his hands around the throat of the guy who had seduced Zoe and somehow convinced her to run away from her home.

Hector had always been a bit rebellious. Nothing serious, but he was a jovial guy who liked to stay out late with his friends. He broke his curfew a lot. Got in trouble for going to parties with alcohol. But it was all normal high school stuff, his parents assured me.

Until he got into bikes. He started hanging out with a new crowd. Bikers. He would be out at all hours and come home wasted. His parents had yelled and tried to discipline him, but that only made it worse.

Both kids had packed their bags and left notes. They had taken money and IDs which was why the cases were unlikely to be kidnappings. Zoe Hammond and Hector Elenes had walked out of their own homes, of their own volition.

To be frank, it wasn't exactly a situation that would have stirred the police into action. There wasn't much they could do. They could ask questions, dig around a bit, but if a sixteen-year-old didn't want to be found, it was easy to disappear. And then in two years, that runaway wouldn't be a kid anymore. It was their life to mess up if they wanted to.

The Hammonds and the Elenes, however, were convinced that something was wrong. They knew their children wouldn't have run away. Even friends had come forward to say that the kids hadn't intended to stay away for good. Even more concerning, no friend had received texts or calls from Zoe or Hector. The police had tried to track their phones, but both of them had been turned off and discarded.

That sent off my alarms more than anything else. A runaway who was angry at their parents was one thing. A teenager who tossed their phone and didn't so much as text their friends? That was quite another.

I had one whole page that listed Hector and Zoe's closest school friends according to their parents. I was going to want to chat with a few of them, especially Zoe's good friend Liz. Girls that age told each other everything. If Zoe was involved with a biker, Liz was going to know details. I was willing to bet that I could get more out of her than the police had.

All Liz had told the police was that Zoe had been seeing an older guy. Zoe had told Liz she was thinking of running away on one occasion, but Liz had never thought Zoe was serious. Liz was concerned for her friend, so I doubted she was trying to hide information. But she probably didn't even know how much knowledge she had. She had probably figured the police wouldn't care about the random gossip from a teenager's sleepover.

I would chat with some of Hector's friends too. Perhaps a smile and a wink from me could get some overeager kid to give me all the information he could think of. But something told me that Liz was the key to this case.

All my other notes were about drug activity in La Playa. The Hammonds and the Elenes had been convinced that bikers were drug dealers. There were rumors of course, but also some compelling evidence and even a few arrests. I would want to push on my contact at the police department to see if there was a high number of biker dealers, or if that was a stereotype.

I hadn't realized it, but Outlaw Souls was fairly well-known. It hadn't taken the parents much to dig up the name of the club.

"These bikers, they know how to avoid getting caught," Mr. Hammond had said. "And they know how to use young girls to move drugs. No one suspects a pony-tailed teen."

I felt the man was a bit dramatic, but I had to admit he had a point. If the bikers were on the radar for drug activity, it would make sense that they would want to recruit some impressionable helpers. Not to mention it wasn't unprecedented to use teenagers.

There had been a big drug bust in LA a few years ago in which a detective discovered cocaine being moved through a college sorority house. It had gone on for years because no one had bothered to look past the shiny pink facade of Beta Kappa Gamma.

On my final page of notes were two other names: Grace Vasquez and Phillip Harding. The Hammonds and Elenes' had explained that those two had also attended West La Playa High School and had run away about a year before.

The parents had reported it, but the investigations had fizzled out. I would have to check, but according to the Hammonds, Grace's parents had pretty much given up on her. She had been a wild child and got involved with a bad crowd. Rumor had it she had been dating a biker dude before she dropped out of school and vanished.

Grace and Zoe had been on the same volleyball team. It was a tenuous connection, but the Hammonds clung to it. Zoe could have been introduced to her mysterious older boyfriend by Grace. Once again, I figured this was something Liz could confirm or deny.

As for Phillip, the only connection was bikes. He had been a known bike-lover. He had even fixed up his own Harley during his senior year. He had been a month away from eighteen when he left his home. His mother, a single mom with three other kids, hadn't even reported it. The name only came up because Hector's friend had mentioned Hector getting in touch with Phillip at some point in the last year.

I sighed as I came to the end of my notes. Between the random dates, lists of names, and theories based on local gossip, it was a tangled web indeed. It's what I had asked for though. By solving this case, I could actually make a difference.

Instead of one cheating scumbag getting his comeuppance (which was satisfying in a small-ball type of way), I could be extricating some poor kid from a drug ring. I could be saving them from jail, addiction, or death. I could be ensuring that the streets of La Playa stayed a little cleaner.

Plus it would feel good. I smiled as I pictured myself busting a drug ring and sending a bunch of no-good guys to jail. I hoped whatever pervert had preyed on a sixteen-year-old girl got the longest sentence.

I had a photo of Zoe taped to one page. She was cute, but visibly young. It was a school photo, her brown eyes wide open and she wore a bashful smile. Zoe was cute, but not the type to get a ton of attention from boys. Her mouth was too wide and she hadn't quite grown into her looks. Her parents had said she could be shy as well and desperate to please others. The exact type of girl that older guys could manipulate.

I tore my eyes away from the photo and snapped my notebook shut. I had thirty minutes until Pin's arrival. I shoved my book into my desk drawer and headed to the bathroom. I ran a hand through my hair and swiped on a layer of pink lip gloss, then surveyed the results in the mirror. I was wearing leggings and a cream cable-knit sweater. My feet were bare.

I wanted to look good, but not like I tried too hard. Pin clearly wanted a hook-up. I had figured he would, but he was the one who came out and suggested a night in.

I hadn't decided if I would sleep with him again. It was a tricky line to walk. For one, I had already slept with him and it had been good. Definitely good enough that I was not averse to repeating the experience.

But would I just be sleeping with him for the case? When it was put that way, it all sounded a little bit grimy. Then again, who cared what methods I used as long as I got results? Plus, there was no guarantee that Pin was involved.

I tried to picture Pin approaching a teenage girl and giving her drugs to carry. It seemed totally out of the question. And I had difficulty imagining that Kim would be cool with that kind of behavior.

I considered Moves or the other guys I had met at the Blue Dog Saloon. I hadn't spent enough time with them to get a gauge. Moves had been friendly, and he did have a certain self-aware charm. Would he use that charm to manipulate a younger girl or perhaps a kid who looked up to him?

As for Kim and Pin, they could be ignorant since it was a bigger club or they could be in denial. It was amazing how people could justify crimes in their heads. People could be so blind when it was convenient. Like maybe Pin hadn't looked too close at a brother's new girl. Maybe he hadn't noticed she was super young because noticing that kind of thing would only keep him up at night or lead to him having to question his friend.

It was possible. If I had learned anything in my time as a PI, it was that anything was possible.

And as a PI, I had to use every resource I had access to. Which was why I hadn't even hesitated to text Pin once I had all the information about the case. He was an easy way into the Outlaw Souls. I could ask around for months before I got intel that Pin could give to me in a day. He had already told me plenty about the club on our fake date.

Pin had said that Outlaw Souls were above dealing drugs or any other illegal activities, but he would have said that no matter what. He handled the money after all, so he was definitely going down if it turned out they were running a drug ring.

I felt a strange prickling at the back of my neck. If a biker club was running a big-scale drug operation, they would need a good accountant. Someone to keep the books looking clean. Someone smart who understood how to make the money disappear, go somewhere safe. Someone to make the books look legit.

Someone like Pin.

I flipped open my notebook and jotted down a few more notes. So far I had interacted with Pin, Moves, and Kim. Pin had mentioned there were almost twenty members in the club, not to mention pledges and family and friends. That was a lot of unknowns.

I put my notebook back into my desk. This time I wouldn't take it out again. I needed to be light and easy around Pin. All the unanswered questions concerning Zoe,

Hector, and the others had to disappear from my face. Pin wasn't going to want to spend an evening with a PI haunted by a multilayered mystery.

He wanted a chill girl. A girl who wouldn't ask him to define the relationship or act too clingy.

I'd gathered that much from our night together, but his leaving in the dead of night had confirmed it. For whatever reason, Pin didn't want to be the morning after guy. That was just fine with me. As long as he didn't suspect that I was investigating his beloved bike club.

Pin came off as a pretty mild and even-tempered guy, but I had no doubt that if he sensed for even a moment that I was prying into biker business, he would be furious. To be honest, I didn't have a plan. I had to own up to that as seven o'clock drew nearer. I was going to have to play it by ear.

The fact of the matter was that Pin might not want to have any sort of conversation with a chick he was hooking up with. And I wasn't sure I could make him pursue me in earnest. I had a healthy self-esteem, but even I knew when a guy didn't want a girlfriend.

Besides, becoming his girlfriend would be going way too far. I just needed to be peripheral. I needed to hang around Pin as much as I could, maybe even go out with him and Kim and other bikers. I needed to drift on the sidelines, cute and approachable, but not a threat at all. I needed to keep my eyes and ears open.

That was the only semblance of a plan I could come up with. All great investigators knew that plans always went to shit anyway. Veronica had a favorite saying: I make a plan, and God laughs.

I would just adapt and think on my feet. To prove my point, I bounced on the balls of my feet and shadowboxed, just to pump myself up.

As if on cue, there was a knock on my door. Pin had arrived.

"It's showtime," I whispered to myself. I put a smile on my face and headed to my door.

As I gripped the door handle in anticipation to see him, the smile started to feel genuine.

THIRTEEN
PIN

She was even prettier than I had remembered. Or she had gotten prettier in the last few days.

Either way, I couldn't help but grin when she opened the door. She was wearing an oversized sweater, her hair loose and slightly tousled. She was ready for a comfy night in, and I loved it. My stomach warmed at the thought of how nice it would be to skip the whole awkward dating phase and get straight to the cuddling on the couch phase.

"Hey," she said.

"I," I said. "I got wine."

She quirked an eyebrow and gave me a saucy grin as she ushered me inside. She shut the door behind me. "I had you pegged as a beer guy."

"Well, I assumed you were a wine girl," I said.

I stood still once I was inside. Memories of the last time I was there rushed to the forefront of my mind. The heat and the tension and how I had lifted her up while she wrapped her legs around my waist. We had both been too tipsy for any awkwardness then, but now I didn't quite know how to stand or where to put the wine I was gripping in one hand.

"Good guess," Claire said. "And you even got red, my favorite."

"I thought about rosé," I said.

Claire let out a little snort. "Don't insult me."

She grabbed the wine and waved one hand towards the couch. "Take a seat. I'll open this and then we can decide on food."

I wandered over to her couch and sat down. After a moment of thought, I scooched forward and took off my leather jacket. I was wearing a worn white T-shirt and jeans. I folded my jacket neatly and placed it on the arm of the couch.

I ran my palm over the smooth dark brown leather and gazed at the maps on the wall. I remembered the maps from the other night, but I hadn't bothered to look at them too closely since I'd been pretty distracted. I scanned them now. California. Europe. A massive world map.

For some reason, the decor made sense for Claire.

She padded across the floor with the open wine in one hand and two glasses in her other hand. I admired her pale little feet as she plopped down on the couch.

"I like your maps," I said.

"Thanks!" She flashed me a grin that made my heart speed up.

"You travel a lot?" I asked.

"No, but I want to," Claire said. "I wanna have a massive map with little pins in every place I've been."

It made sense. She was an adventurer at heart. "You from California originally?"

I cringed at the question. I had been eager to skip

dating, but somehow I still asked the most typical First Date Question.

"Yeah, up north though," Claire said. "I fled to LA as soon as I could."

"Why?" I asked.

She shrugged and tucked her feet up under her, leaning closer as she did. I caught the scent of her shampoo, a combination of mint and florals.

"I wanted excitement I guess," she said. "I thought LA would be big and glitzy like the movies."

"And it let you down?" I asked.

Claire frowned. She leaned forward and poured two glasses of wine. "Everything lets me down eventually. But I still get my hopes up about the next thing."

She handed me a glass and I took a sip. I didn't usually drink wine, but I hadn't wanted to show up with a six-pack of Budweisers. Claire would have been game, but it would have felt too much like a night with the brothers. Claire was anything but a leather-clad biker dude.

"What about you?" she asked. "What's your story?"

"La Playa born and raised," I said. "Not much of a story."

"You're an accountant in a notorious biker club," Claire said. "You've gotta have stories."

She raised her glass to her lips and peered at me with her massive blue eyes as she took a sip.

"I guess it's the norm for me," I said. "The bikers are all I've ever known."

"But why did you join?" she asked.

I frowned at the space in front of me. I hadn't expected to get deep life questions, but I didn't mind. From any other chick I was hooking up with, I would have been annoyed. I would have wanted to cut it with the deep history and emotional reasoning and just get to the physical.

But I liked the way Claire asked as if she really wanted to know, just to know. She wasn't asking to fill the silence or to be polite. She had a burning curiosity, and it was directed at me. I was flattered.

"I wanted a family I guess," I said.

I shocked myself at my own honesty and felt an instant wave of embarrassment. I didn't want to be a mopy guy talking about all his baggage.

"Not that I don't have a family," I said. "I have my mom, and she's great, I just wanted more camaraderie I guess. I never had any siblings by blood."

Claire nodded with eagerness. "Me neither. I used to pretend I had like 7 brothers and sisters, I would even make up names and personalities for all of them."

I had an image of a tiny blonde Claire carrying on an imaginary argument with an invisible sibling and smiled. "Which one was your favorite?"

"I had this awesome older brother," Claire said. "Once we hopped into train cars and rode the rails like they used to do in the olden days."

"That's sort of why I got into bikes," I said. "I wanted to be able to just take off with my good friends and go anywhere."

Claire's eyes turned dreamy, and she let out a little sigh. "It sounds lovely."

"It is," I said.

There was a beat of silence in which we simply locked eyes. It wasn't uncomfortable though. It was more like we were seeing each other for who we were, in the light of the day, away from a dance club or a bar or fancy restaurant.

"Well, enough about the residual scars of childhood," Claire said with a wry grin. "What should we eat?"

In a matter of minutes, Claire produced an array of take-out menus. To my delight, she had anecdotes and reviews about nearly every single one. One place had great pizza, but it was a long wait. A Thai food restaurant was her go-to on lazy Sundays.

I laughed at all of Claire's pithy comments. At last, we opted for Chinese food. I was happy to discover that Claire and I had the same philosophy when it came to ordering Chinese food. We selected several dishes and didn't worry about having too much since we could always eat leftovers. We ordered sesame chicken, dumplings, fried rice, crab rangoon, and beef with broccoli.

Once we had placed the order, I felt myself relaxing around Claire. She was easy to be around, and it was clear that she wasn't uncomfortable. She flicked on the TV and we surfed the channels for a while, but mostly we just chatted about our respective jobs and friends and living in La Playa. I told Claire that Kim was recovering quite nicely as she described her colleague, Veronica.

"I have to ask," Claire said. "What is the deal with Moves?"

I laughed at her bemused expression. "He's simultaneously the best and the worst."

"I mean, when he dragged me over that first night, I had no idea what was going on," Claire said. "Obviously, I went with it, 'cause I was pursuing Trey, but I swear no one has ever wingmanned with such confidence."

"Confident, yes," I said. "But not subtle."

"I mean, I guess it kinda worked in the end," Claire said.

I looked up with a start. It was the first time either one

of us had referenced the night we had spent just a few yards away, in her bedroom.

"Not really thanks to Moves though," I said.

"I'm sure he would disagree," she said.

"Yeah, he would," I said.

I shook my head and smiled over my friend. "He's a good guy though."

"Yeah, definitely charming," she said.

"Don't let that fool you," I said. "There are a lot of guys in East La Playa that would *not* call Moves charming."

Claire furrowed her brow in puzzlement.

"He's our enforcer," I said.

"So he's, like, your muscle?" she asked.

I shrugged. "He's the one who makes sure enemies stay in line. He's a fighter."

"Oh." Claire didn't look horrified or judgmental. Just curious once again. "I didn't know everyone had roles."

"Not the newer members, but most of us do, yeah," I said.

Most people who weren't familiar with biker clubs were surprised at our organization. Most outsiders figured we just fucked around on our bikes, but it took structure to keep a club going strong.

"But obviously the accountant is the most badass," Claire said. "Even more badass than the enforcer."

I grinned at her sarcasm. I liked how she was game to joke about anything and everything.

"Technically, my official title is Treasurer," I said, matching her mocking tone.

"Oh, I'm sorry, Mr. Treasurer," Claire said.

Just then her phone rang and Claire leapt up with a cry that the food had arrived. The next few minutes were a flurry of opening all the dishes and filling our plates.

What would it be like, I found myself wondering, to spend every evening like this? Not bad, I realized. It wouldn't be bad at all.

I peered over at Claire as she wielded her chopsticks like an expert to scoop up a pork dumpling. Once we had settled back on the couch with our food, Claire started flipping through the TV channels again.

"Wait, stop!" I cried out. "It's Shark Tank!"

"Really?" she asked.

"It's amazing," I said. "I watched it once when I was home sick, and now I'm addicted."

The episode featured a few guys who had designed a special kind of surfboard.

"They are so bad at public speaking," Claire said.

"Yeah, they'll never get an offer," I said. "Being able to sell yourself is just as important as the product."

One episode bled into another, and pretty soon we were both offering our opinions on business products as if we were the experts. During one commercial break, we cleared up the dishes and put away the leftover food. During another one, we refilled our wine glasses.

Somehow, we ended up sitting closer. I had my legs out in front of me and one arm slung over the back of the couch while Claire sat cross-legged, her one knee grazing my thigh. When I was done with my wine, I leaned forward and placed it on the coffee table. As I leaned back, I grazed Claire's knee with my fingers, as gently as I could. I looked up to see how she had responded.

Her company was nice (even better than I had thought it would be), but I had come over for a reason. Claire gave me a small smile and leaned even closer. She shifted herself until she had turned on the couch and was facing me. I reached up and placed my hand on her neck.

I could see the wine had stained the inside of her lips a deep red.

Her lips brushed mine, soft and sweet, and I pulled her closer. It was different kissing her sober. In fact, it was better. I was able to feel more and taste more. I was hyper aware of her soft and full lower lip, and the gentle sighs escaping from her mouth. Every second seemed so filled with sensation.

There was no frenzy like before. No rush to go all the way before we missed our chance. We enjoyed ourselves, and we went slowly.

After a long while, I pulled away to see that Claire had somehow wormed her way into my lap, her legs hanging over my far leg. My arms were wrapped around her waist, and her warm torso was pressed against my chest.

She blinked up at me and smiled. "You wanna watch more Shark Tank?"

And so we did, but Claire stayed ensconced in my arms.

"So what would you invent?" she asked. "For Shark Tank."

"Probably a cleaning product," I said. "Those always do pretty well."

"But that's boring," Claire said. "Also you have to be specific."

"I don't know enough about cleaning," I said.

"Ugh, you would never get an offer." I could tell she was smiling even though she was faced away from me; I could sense it.

"What would you invent?" I asked.

"Maybe a home lie detector test," Claire said. "So all the desperate wives who hire me can just scan their husbands with an app and know they're full of bull."

"How would that even work?" I asked.

"I dunno, I would hire engineers or computer scientists to figure it out," she said.

Sometimes we would kiss a bit, sometimes just watch. It went on like that for a while, and eventually the combination of kissing, wine, and Chinese food lulled me into a drowsy state of peace.

Before I knew it, I was on my back and drifting off to sleep, Claire dozing against my chest.

FOURTEEN
CLAIRE

I was surprised by how the night with Pin went, but I was happy with it all. It felt right. Right for me and right for the case. It was bad that I was conflating my interests with an investigation, but I could worry about that later after I had tracked down the missing kids.

When I woke up in his arms on the couch, sunlight trickling through the shades, I didn't get up right away. I was so comfortable, and his chest was so warm as if there was a compact furnace beneath his skin.

Then I pushed myself up and padded towards the bathroom. I touched my neck and massaged a crick from the awkward sleeping position. Next time, we were totally getting to the bed.

I stared at myself in the mirror. I was so sure there would be a next time. I was looking forward to the next time. And it wasn't just because of the case.

Pin and I got along. Yes, we already had chemistry as demonstrated by the night out with Kim, but last night had been more than just physical attraction. He was easy to talk to, but also interesting. I couldn't quite figure him out.

I peeked out of the bathroom to study his sleeping form. He didn't snore, I noted with glee. He just breathed heavily, his chest rising with each inhale. I shook my head and ducked into my bedroom. Watching a sleeping male was a particular brand of obsessive that I did not want to be a part of.

I reminded myself to focus. After all, what had I learned last night? The club was like family for Pin. That kind of thing sounds cute on the surface, but not when you think about all the twisted contracts involved in a family. People committed all manner of sins for family. And they'll do anything to hide the sins of their family too.

I had also learned that Moves was the enforcer. A fighter. Violence seethed beneath his charming smiles. That had shocked me, and I'm not easily surprised.

The bikers had freedom. That's what Pin had meant, I thought, when he spoke about being able to just get on his bike and ride somewhere with his brothers. That part had sounded nice honestly. But not nice enough to make me forget that teenagers were missing and someone was responsible.

I hadn't learned much else about the club. I had gained a lot more intel on Pin. Like he was raised by a single mother, but there was some tension there. I had seen it in his eyes. He liked Shark Tank and was funny too. And a good kisser, but then I had known that before. The other bikers were like his blood.

I sighed and started to change my clothes. There was really only one thing to be done. I had to spend more time with Pin and gain his trust. That was the only way I was going to learn more about Outlaw Souls. I couldn't complain. I was going to enjoy spending time with Pin. In fact, it was possible that I was going to have too much fun.

When I emerged from my bedroom, he was sitting up on the couch, blinking the sleep from his eyes. He ran one hand through his rumpled hair, and my stomach somersaulted. God, he was cute in the morning.

"Hi," I said.

"Hey," he said. "Sorry I stayed the night."

"It's ok," I said. "It was nice even."

"I know, but I didn't mean to." His mouth had pressed into a stern line as if he was mad at himself. I didn't want him to beat himself up. I had wanted him to stay.

I flashed a sunny smile as I walked over. "Then let's pretend that you left and then just came back really early."

That made him chuckle. I was getting good at cheering him up. He had trust issues, that was clear. He didn't like getting close to anyone, especially in a romantic way. I was going to have to get him to let down his walls just a little bit if I was ever going to gain useful information about the club. Being able to make him smile was a good start. We had a ways to go, but I did love a challenge.

"Alright," Pin said. "I came back early to make you breakfast."

"Really?" I asked.

"Of course," he said. "Where's your frying pan? I'll make eggs."

He stood up and headed towards my kitchen with a downright sexy confidence. I was a terrible cook. I lived off of microwave meals and takeout leftovers. I showed Pin the frying pan and told him he could have free reign of my fridge. He pulled out the eggs, grabbed some onions, tomatoes, and cheese and then set to work.

I decided I would make coffee since that was the one culinary thing that I could do quite well. I watched Pin while I scooped the grinds into my machine. He was so tall and muscled, but he looked comfortable over a stovetop. The amount of focus he gave to dicing onions was endearing.

"So when did you pick up your cooking skills?" I asked.

"Ok, I don't have skills," Pin said. "I just know how to make a few solid dishes. Breakfast omelet, pasta with sauce, chicken and pesto. That kind of thing."

"That's more than I know," I said.

Pin gave me a wry look. "I'm not surprised after I saw the random sweaters in your oven."

"It's ideal storage space!" I protested.

Pin just shook his head and continued his work. We sat down at my small table to eat, and I had to give him credit. The eggs scrambled up with the onions, cheese and tomatoes were amazing. I told him as much.

"Would have been better with bacon or ham," he said.

"Next time." I didn't miss his pleased expression at the idea of a next time.

"Your coffee is good too," he said.

"Thank you," I said.

After we had finished eating, we cleaned up. It was nice, but it was getting all a bit humdrum. I had never acted like this much of a married couple with a guy I had just met. I was wondering what came next. Did we just say goodbye? Or were we going to make plans?

Pin lingered over drying the final dish. He pursed his lips as if he was trying to make a tough decision. At last, he spoke. "So have you ever ridden a bike before?"

"No," I said. "They're just so loud and I never knew anyone who had one."

"Mine's outside now," Pin said. "Wanna ride somewhere?"

A giddy surge of excitement rose within me and I clapped my hands in excitement. "Really? Right now?"

"Sure," Pin said. "I always have an extra helmet, and you don't need to worry, I'm an experienced rider."

I was practically hopping from foot to foot with anticipation. I was born a thrill-seeker, so I never said no to something that might give me a rush of adrenaline. I had tried skydiving, rock climbing, and plenty of cliff jumps. But a motorcycle was unexplored territory.

"Ok, what shoes should I wear?" I asked. "I don't own a leather jacket, is that ok?"

"Sneakers or boots are fine," he said, chuckling at my rapid questions. "And a leather jacket is not required. Just wear something sturdy that will protect you from the wind."

I let out a little cry of excitement and ran to my room to get a jacket and shoes. I had abandoned my cool girl detective visage, but I couldn't help it. He probably thought I was a total dork.

When we went outside to the bike, Pin gave me a quick rundown of all the parts. The brakes, gas, gears. I appreciated the lesson. I wouldn't have wanted to just get plopped onto a machine without knowing how it worked.

When he was done with the explanation, Pin got on the bike and told me to hop on behind. I made sure the helmet was secure before sliding into place and wrapping my arms around Pin's chest.

Not even my glee over the motorbike could make me unaware of how close we were, with my chest pressed against his back. It felt good, like I was about to be hurled into the unknown, but I had Pin as a life raft.

Then with a huge rattle of noise, the bike came to life. I gripped Pin even harder as he pushed the bike out onto the road. Then we were off, accelerating faster than I thought possible.

The rush hit me even harder than I had expected. As we picked up more and more speed, I felt like I had left all the pesky heavy parts of my body behind on the curb. As if my body had been reduced just to movement, so it could run as fast as my spirit.

I gripped Pin's jacket in my fists and let out a yelp of joy. The wind yanked the noise out of my throat, and even that gave me another jolt of adrenaline.

Then I leaned my head against Pin's upper back and closed my eyes, just letting the sensations wash over me. It was different from skydiving. The rush was more contained and controlled. It felt safer, but the feeling that you were free and alive was the same.

When I opened my eyes, I saw that we were riding along the coast, the beach stretching in front of us as far as we could see. I soaked in the view from this new vantage point.

Pin pulled into a small lot by the boardwalk and parked. I jumped off the bike and pulled the helmet from my head. My hair was probably a mess from being stuck under the big black helmet, but I didn't care. "That was incredible!"

"You liked it?" Pin asked.

"Liked it? I loved it," I said.

He grinned at my obvious joy. "I thought you might."

"Seriously, I'm this close to buying one secondhand," I said. "My parents would flip if they ever found out, but that felt too good."

"You're such an adrenaline junkie," Pin said. "I can't believe you never tried a bike before."

I shrugged. "I just didn't think I was a biker person."

It was the truth plain and simple. I had never seen a

group of bikers and thought, "Ah, yes, now that's where I belong." But one ride behind Pin had me rethinking that.

"You might need some lessons before you're ready for your own bike," Pin said. "I'm happy to teach you."

I threw my arms out to show how ready I was. "When can we start?"

Pin reached out and grabbed one of my hands, seemingly on impulse. He pulled me close to him and placed a big kiss on my lips. It was a fun quick kiss. The kind of kiss you gave your significant other in public, just because you can't help yourself.

He pulled back, and I smiled to let him know I was ok with it. He kept holding my hand as he led me towards the boardwalk.

"That's one of my favorite rides," Pin said. "I like to have the highway under me and the ocean to my side."

"It was beautiful," I said.

"And there's a place over here that has the best ice cream," he said.

The sun was out, and it was the perfect day for ice cream. I never would have guessed that a mint chocolate chip cone tasted best after riding several miles on the bike of a bike with a helmet making you sweat. Pin and I sat on a bench and enjoyed our cones.

When I was a little girl, my parents would ask me what I wanted to do with my free time. I would wake up on a Saturday, and my mother would say, "What should we do today?" My dad would say, "You pick our activity."

And every single time I would answer the same way: "Something we've never done before."

My parents would get frustrated. They would want me to come up with specifics, but I didn't have specific plans in mind, I just wanted something new.

"What about the park?" my dad would say. "You like the park."

"Or we could do finger painting," my mom would say. "You enjoyed that last time."

They were right. I did like the park. I did like finger painting. But I had already done those things.

I don't know why I thought of that sitting next to Pin near the beach. And once I remembered, I started to wonder when my parents had just stopped bothering to ask. Them not asking hadn't changed anything. I still knew what I wanted.

The question tickling the back of my mind was if it might be ok to do the same thing more than once with a person who was interesting enough to make every single time feel different. Because, maybe, I did want to take another ride with Pin. And maybe I would be more than happy to take the same route and get off at the same boardwalk and go get the same ice cream. If it was with Pin.

I sighed and stared out over the waves. They were a deep blue today, and the tips sparkled and gleamed like buried treasure. That question was not going to be answered in one day.

"Penny for your thoughts?" Pin asked.

I glanced up at him through my lashes. "They're not for sale."

Then I reached over and grabbed his hand and just held it in mine. I would start worrying about the investigation later. I would wonder about what feelings were real and which emotions were just part of the case.

I would think about all that later.

For now, I just wanted to be a girl sitting with a guy, after a pretty amazing date.

FIFTEEN

PIN

A perfect hook-up was one thing. A perfect evening spent watching TV and chatting, while harder to come by, was still possible.

But a perfect hook-up, followed by a perfect evening, followed by a perfect morning? I was starting to wonder if Claire could be real.

After I dropped Claire back at her place, I headed home. I didn't mess around this time. I knew I was going to want to see her again. For sex, maybe, but also just to be with her. So I texted her right away that I had a great time, and would like to do it again. Kim had been right about that. Claire wasn't the girl you played games with.

Claire had answered she was busy with work stuff, but she could maybe do dinner the day after next. That was good. It gave me time to think over what was happening because it wasn't casual anymore.

Things had shifted during our evening of chatting and watching TV. Or maybe they had changed while we slept, fully clothed, in each other's arms. Or perhaps things with

Claire had been different from the moment we met, and I had just been in denial.

I couldn't push it to the side anymore and tell myself that Claire was just another girl to hook up with. I had always known she could be dangerous, but now I had to admit that I was officially in danger of falling for her hard.

The thing was, the thought of falling no longer filled me with fear and revulsion. I didn't have terrifying images of Claire worming her way into my heart only to break it. I didn't foresee a future of cheating and betrayal.

Instead, I saw lazy afternoons curled up with Claire on her couch. I saw us planning long bike trips. I could see us celebrating anniversaries and even moving in together. It was reckless to think that way, but I couldn't help myself. The crazy thing was, it didn't even bother me. I didn't feel like I was letting myself down or being weak. I felt good. For the first time in a long time, I believed in something.

At the same time, my cold and practical side knew that this was huge. A lifetime of philosophy on love and relationships was being tossed out the window. And yes, it felt good, but that didn't mean it was good. Or maybe it was good now, but would it be good in six months? Or a year?

Whenever my mom met a new guy, things were always good. Sure, I saw the red flags, but my mother never did. It was a chilling thought, but maybe I was in my mother's shoes. Maybe there were red flags all over Claire, and I just couldn't see them. I was blind.

I pictured Claire, her eyes big and gleaming as she looked at me right before we kissed. I heard the way she talked about her work, with jokes and sly phrases, but I could still tell she cared about what she did. I imagined the way her mouth quirked at the edges when she talked about all the adventures she wanted to have and places she wanted to travel.

There were no red flags in sight. Claire was smart and funny and charming. Not to mention gorgeous. I couldn't obsess over Claire anymore. It was getting pathetic. I grabbed my phone and texted Moves:

Drinks at Blue Dog? 6?

He responded right away telling me that he would be there. That was the best thing about Moves. He never turned down a drink.

When I got there, I grabbed a beer and headed straight for a table in the corner. I knew that Moves could happily set up shop at the center table and start holding court, but I wanted a more private conversation.

Moves walked in and made a beeline for the table. Once we had settled in with our drinks, Moves looked me in the eye and raised his brows. "So? What's going on?"

"How do you know something is going on?"

"Because you look practically giddy," Moves said.

I rolled my eyes. However I looked, I knew it wasn't giddy.

"Seriously, tell me," Moves said.

"I've been seeing this chick," I said.

Moves was never one for underreaction. He slammed his palm flat on the table and let out a whoop. Then he leaned back and gave a low whistle.

"You, Pin Gallegos, are actually seeing someone?" he asked. "Not hooking up, not just doing casual hang-outs with?"

I rolled my eyes. "Ok, ok I've been single for a while."

"Not single," Moves said. "Anti-love."

"I am not anti-love," I said. "You can't be anti-something if it doesn't exist."

"Jesus," Moves muttered.

"Ok, ok," I said. "Can I just get back to the current issue, I could use your advice."

Moves perked up at that. "But of course. The master is always happy to help the apprentice."

I took a swig of beer. "I would not call you a master. But I will admit, you have more faith in relationships than I do."

Moves nodded.

"And I guess I wanna know why?" I asked. "None of your relationships have worked out, but despite a string of failures, you're still ready to dive into the next one?"

"Right," Moves said. "I feel like I just got insulted."

I shrugged and studied the table. I didn't mean to call Moves' past relationships failures, but he'd had five girlfriends in the last five years. Every single one, he had called his soul mate. I wanted to know how he had gone from soulmates to nothing. And I wanted to know how he got back up and kept moving after each relationship that he had wanted to last forever ended.

"Don't know how else to ask it," I said.

Moves pressed his mouth into a firm line and furrowed his brow. "S'alright. You may have a point."

"I just don't know how to trust a relationship," I said. "I trusted one once, a long time ago. Didn't end well."

"Ok, but trust is so boring," Moves said.

I gave him a quizzical look. Everyone knew that trust was the cornerstone of a healthy relationship and all that sappy stuff.

"It's not just about trust," Moves said. "Don't get me wrong, trust is a big part of it, but it's about something more. It's more fun and exciting than that."

"I don't get it," he said.

"You say you don't have fun with this girl?" Moves asked.

"Of course I do," I said.

"So enjoy that first," Moves said. "You don't have to go straight to the heavy stuff."

"I just don't see how I can *not* consider all the heavy stuff," I said, drumming my fingers atop the table as I contemplated. "The heavy stuff is what'll bite you in the ass eventually, right?"

"But the fun stuff and the stuff that makes you care about her in the first place." Moves shook his head and waved his hand for emphasis. "That's what gets you through the tough times."

Moves leaned back and smiled, happy with his conclusion. I sighed.

Moves had a point. I was still scared as hell about everything that could go wrong with Claire. But the feeling of comfort and excitement I got when I was around her made me forget about the danger and tragedy that the future could hold.

I gave Moves a nod. I would think about his philosophy. I couldn't make him any promises though. Moves leaned forward and clapped his hand on my shoulder. "When in doubt, just take it one step at a time."

"One step at a time, huh?" I asked. "That's tough for me."

"Why?" Moves asked.

"I just keep thinking about what's gonna happen at step 200 or 300," I said.

Moves shrugged. "I never think ahead. Maybe I should."

We both laughed and finished our drinks.

"Invite her to the club barbecue this week," Moves said.

I looked up in alarm. It was no joke to invite someone to a club social event. It meant I was willing to introduce Claire to all the most important people in my life.

Then again, when I pictured walking into that barbecue with Claire at my side, a warm feeling spread through me. It would feel right, I realized, to introduce her to my brothers and their girls. I wanted to see her joke with Ryder and ask Raul about learning to ride.

She would fit right in as well. Claire wouldn't be hesitant or shy around the bikers. They couldn't faze her. She was undaunted by pretty much everything. In fact, she would relish meeting the guys and asking for good stories.

"Alright," I said. "I think I will."

"Awesome," Moves said. "Can't wait to meet her."

I nearly choked on my swig of beer as I remembered. "Oh, you have."

"What?" Moves asked. He sat straight up at this news. "When?"

I smiled and enjoyed Moves' befuddlement. "Here actually."

Moves' eyes widened as it dawned on him.

"No fucking way," he said. "The blonde chick the other night?"

"Yup," I said.

"Ok, so I'm definitely your best man?" Moves asked.

I rolled my eyes. Inviting Claire to the Outlaw Souls barbecue was one thing; getting married was quite another.

Despite my dismissal, Moves made several more jokes. I let him go on for a while because I was feeling appreciative, but when I was done with my beer I stood up and said goodbye.

When I got back to my place, I typed out a message to Claire:

Biker barbecue this weekend, you wanna come?

Her response came in minutes:

Yes! Perfect opportunity to find someone to teach me to ride!

I grinned at her enthusiasm and texted back:

You think I'm not good enough?

She fired back in no time:

Oh, I like to keep my options open.

For the rest of the evening, I couldn't stop smiling.

SIXTEEN
CLAIRE

I couldn't believe my luck. Pin was full of information, but I couldn't come out and ask him if he was in any way, shape, or form involved with illicit drug activity. A barbecue with all the bikers would be different. I wouldn't even have to ask, I could just observe. I could pick up plenty of details about the other Outlaw Souls and their habits. I would gain so much more intel than could be picked up on a casual date with Pin.

Because I had to admit that we were dating now. Whatever was between us, it was not just casually hanging out with mixed intentions. There was something new and very delicate growing.

I couldn't think about that though. I had to separate my pesky feelings from the case. And going to the barbecue was definitely the best choice for the case.

If I was really lucky, Zoe or Hector would be there. Maybe tucked into the host's house or sitting on the edges looking nervous. I didn't think this case was going to be that easy though. After a few days of digging through the details of Zoe and Hector's disappearances and interviewing friends, the case was only growing murkier and murkier.

I responded to Pin's invite as quickly as I could and then set my phone aside. It gave me a warm feeling in my stomach to text him, and it was too easy to fall into the trap of texting him back and forth for an hour. We had done that yesterday. I sighed and turned to my notes.

I wanted to have a firm grasp on everything I knew before the barbecue that weekend. Any random little fact might help. I could think of a thousand ways a biker might give away what happened to the teenagers without actually coming out and telling me.

I flipped to my page with notes from my chat with Liz. I had tracked her down the afternoon after Pin slept over, and my hunch had paid off. Liz was a wealth of information. I just had to approach her from the right angle.

Instead of ambushing her at school, I had texted her an explanation of who I was and what I wanted. Zoe's parents had already told Liz that they were hiring a PI, so Liz agreed to meet me at a coffee shop after she was done with school for the day.

Liz was a nervous girl. From the second she sat down in the seat across from me at the table I had selected in the corner of the shop, she was fidgeting. She tugged at the hairbands on her wrist and fiddled with the ends of her mousy brown hair. I gave her a big smile to try and put her at ease, but it didn't seem to help. It made me wonder if she had always been this way, or if she had changed after Zoe left.

"I don't really know if I can help that much," Liz said. "I already told everything I could think of to the police."

"That's ok," I said. "Honestly, I just want some insight into Zoe as a person, and I figured you would be the best one for that."

"Oh." Liz blinked three times as if it had never occurred to her that someone might want to know about Zoe's personality or characteristics. I didn't blame her. Our society has a strange habit of misunderstanding and misrepresenting teenage girls.

Liz took a dainty sip of her caramel latte and then set it down. She chewed on her lower lip as she thought. "Her parents could probably describe Zoe better than me."

I did my best to not roll my eyes. I had great sympathy for everything a junior high school girl goes through on a daily basis, but I couldn't stand low self-esteem. If Liz spent her whole life discounting her knowledge and words before she even said anything, then no one was ever going to listen to her.

"I'm sure Zoe kept a few secrets." I gave Liz a conspiratory smile. "We don't tell our parents everything, right?"

Most times, I hate that I look so young. It's harder to get taken seriously. But in this case, I wanted Liz to see me as a friend. Not a parent. Not a police officer. I wanted her to think of me as someone just a few years older than she was. I had even worn skinny jeans and leopard-print ballet flats to try and look a bit more hip.

Instead of leaning forward to gossip with me, Liz just lifted one shoulder and let it drop. "It was just the guy she was dating. But she didn't even tell me that much about him."

This was a sore spot. I could tell by the way Liz looked down, it had hurt when Zoe had shut her out all those months ago. The wound was still tender. I could use that.

"Yeah, I heard about him," I said. "She only told you that he was older, right?"

"I saw a text on her phone and asked," Liz said. "She

told me he was older and they had to keep it on the down low."

"See, that's odd to me." I tapped my finger against my lower lip in a show of thinking. "I would think Zoe would wanna brag *all* about her new boyfriend."

I widened my eyes and shook my head, as if I was so over girls who boasted about their boyfriends. Liz mirrored my annoyance in an instant. I had played it right.

"Yeah, I mean, I don't even know if he was actually her boyfriend," Liz said. "To be honest, it seemed like he was using her."

I leaned forward and raised my brows. Everyone loves to gossip. You just have to direct them to the right topic. "To deal drugs? Did she ever mention that?"

"Oh, no," Liz said. "I never heard her say anything about drugs, I just meant it seemed like he was using her to make an ex jealous or something. Like, I got the idea he was not as into Zoe as she was into him."

"How did you get that idea?" I asked.

"Well, Zoe would get really moody," Liz said. "She would be on her phone all the time and, when I peeked over her shoulder, I would see that she was texting him but he wasn't texting her back. It drove her crazy, but then eventually he would get in touch with her and she would be all smiles until it started over again in a few days."

"You're observant," I said. "You'd make a good PI."

Liz smiled up at me. Poor girl probably didn't get enough praise. Liz wasn't an athlete, nor was she a great beauty, and she didn't have brains galore. She was just average. Overlooked by boys and adults. Now her one friend had vanished as well.

"Can you tell me anything else you noticed about him or the relationship?" I asked.

Liz pressed her lips together and looked at the ceiling as she thought. She was really thinking at this point, not just giving me basic answers.

"Well, he was a biker," she said.

"How do you know that?" I asked.

Liz shrugged. "Zoe started wearing a leather jacket that he gave her. She mentioned him taking her on a few rides."

I leaned forward with eagerness. "Did the jacket have a patch sewed on?"

"No," Liz said.

An Outlaw Souls patch would have been all too obvious. I nodded. Then I leaned back and gave Liz a careful look.

"I know this might be awkward to ask," I said. "But I do feel I need to know now if Zoe was sexually active with this guy. Do you know if she was?"

Liz's cheeks turned pink. It was a safe bet that she was a virgin. It didn't mean Zoe was, but I filed the information away.

"She had condoms," Liz said. She lowered her voice to a tiny whisper on the last word. "But I'm not sure."

"Ok, thanks for telling me," I said.

"He also had a scar," Liz said. "I never met him, but Zoe mentioned how he had this scar on his cheek from a fight he had gotten in and it was really hot or something."

I nodded. As if this case wasn't dramatic enough, now the main villain had a signature scar.

That was all I got from Liz when it came to the facts of the case, but at least it was something. She gave me plenty more context as well. She described Zoe as being really nice and kind-hearted, almost a pushover. Zoe had grown a little more glum and irritated when she started seeing the mysterious older guy, but she had always apologized to Liz after snapping at her.

Zoe was a people-pleaser, I realized as I skimmed my notes. She wanted to make everyone happy. It sounds nice, but it's a surefire way to get manipulated. Especially if you end up in the wrong pair of arms.

Liz had been sad about Zoe. She missed her best friend. Something told me that Liz had been missing Zoe since before she even ran away. Zoe had become distant when she got involved with the biker, isolating herself. It was a classic tale. Get a young person away from all their friends, make them depend on you, and then they'll do anything you say.

As for Hector, I still didn't have much. I had chatted with a few of his friends who had confirmed what his parents told me. He got really into bikes. Started cutting class. Grew distant. Then one day he was gone.

His friends had seemed confused when I asked about drugs. I wanted to know if Hector had dabbled in anything before. They blinked before slowly nodding.

"Not marijuana," I said. "I'm talking heroin or cocaine."

Their little teenage eyes had bugged out of their heads, which was confirmation that Hector had not been shooting up, at least not in front of them.

I lifted my pen and jotted down the date of the barbecue. It was the day after next. I had an urge to invite Pin over. I wanted to see him. We could watch TV and chat, and it would take my mind off the case.

Except that was bad. Pin was part of the case. When I saw Pin, I should be thinking of the case, not the way his smile was ever-so-slightly crooked or the way he looked right into my eyes when I was talking.

Or how much I wanted to sleep with him again. I was happy we hadn't gone further than kissing the last time we saw each other, but I couldn't deny I had the urge to go further. I wanted to know what it would be like now that I knew Pin a bit better.

It was a distraction though. And it was dangerous to yearn for Pin like this.

I decided I would tell him I was busy with work tonight and tomorrow. I would wait until the barbecue to see him again. That way, I could use the time apart to cool down. I would let my little crush fade.

Only, as I put away my notebook and prepared for bed, I worried that it wasn't just a crush. I could tell myself over and over that the barbecue was going to be a reconnaissance mission. It was going to be crucial for my investigation into Outlaw Souls.

But when I thought about the barbecue, I just got excited to spend more time with Pin. And when I pushed aside the excitement, I only felt guilt. I was using him. He thought we were just starting to date. That we had innocent motives and clear intentions.

Before I met Pin, I would have said I was willing to do anything to solve a case. I would lie, beg, borrow or steal in the name of an investigation. Now I wasn't so sure if I was capable of that.

Now it felt like I was about to cross a line.

SEVENTEEN

PIN

When Claire showed up at my place before the barbecue, I almost suggested we bail on the whole thing. I took one look at her in her relaxed-fit green dress paired with combat boots, and I wanted to pull her into my bedroom and keep her there for a solid twenty-four hours.

Instead, I wrapped my arm around her waist and kissed her. I didn't care that we still hadn't defined our relationship or this was technically only our second date. I couldn't resist.

To my joy, she kissed me back with enthusiasm. When she slid her fingers into my hair, I nearly threw away all my self-control. After extending the kiss for a few moments, I pulled back to gaze down into Claire's glowing face.

Her eyes were big and full of mischief, as if it was the funniest joke that I had kissed her before speaking, and her lips were slightly swollen.

"Hi," I said.

"Hey," she said.

"You look good," I said.

"I wasn't sure how to dress for a biker barbecue." She

stepped back to look down at her polka-dot dress. "I almost went with Daisy Dukes and bright red lipstick. Isn't that what biker chicks wear?"

"Nah," I said. "You're perfect the way you are."

She froze at the compliment. I hadn't meant to be so intense, but it just came out. It was true, anyway. Everything about her from the tiny freckles on her nose to her black combat boots was amazing.

"Thank you," Claire murmured.

I shrugged and grabbed her hand. "Should we go?"

"Yeah, I'm ready," Claire said, adjusting her large purse on her shoulder and following me to the door.

"We're just gonna take a car over," I said.

"No bike today?" Claire asked.

"I'm gonna have some beer at the barbecue," I said. "I don't drink and drive."

The barbecue was being held in the parking lot behind Blue Dog Saloon. We had gatherings like this at least once a month. A few of the guys would drag out grills and make hot dogs and burgers. We started in the afternoon, but usually the barbecue lasted long into the night. It wasn't much, but it was my family.

As Claire and I walked up to the parking lot, a flurry of nerves rose up in my stomach. I had never so much as flirted with a girl at a biker barbecue. And I had certainly never brought a date. I hooked up with girls who were far removed from the biker world. I would never bring them to meet my brothers because there was no point. The Outlaw Souls were long-term only.

Yet here I was, walking into the barbecue hand in hand with Claire. Even before we reached the tables in the center of the lot, I could feel eyes on us.

Then Claire squeezed my hand a bit. I looked down to

see her smiling up at me, and the tension in my chest eased in a heartbeat. As we approached a table, Moves appeared at my side. He reached out to shake Claire's hand with a wicked grin.

"I did not think I would ever see you again," Moves said.

I rolled my eyes, but Claire laughed, and the sound made me want to laugh as well.

"Don't worry, I'm not scared off by sub-par wingmen that easily," Claire said.

Moves blinked in surprise. "Fair enough."

A flurry of black leather and dark hair appeared at Claire's side.

"Kim!" Claire said. "It's good to see you."

"Girl, we need to talk," Kim said. "I clearly need to catch up on a lot."

With that, Kim pulled Claire away from me and over to a table. I watched her go with pride. Claire could fit in with the Outlaw Souls. Kim and Moves already adored her. She was different from us in many ways, but there was something in her spirit that we all recognized.

"Jesus, Pin," Moves said. "You've got it bad."

I focused back on Moves. I couldn't deny his point, so I just shrugged.

"I have to say, I do like her for you," Moves said. "Can't really put my finger on it, but it works."

He shrugged and made a move towards the food table. I followed. Claire could chat with Kim, and I would get her a plate of food and a beer.

Moves was right. There was something about Claire that just made sense. She was never going to be an obvious choice. I thought Claire was gorgeous, but she wasn't the type to walk into a room and have all heads turn. Her legs were too short, her clothes were too simple, and she moved just a little too quickly to the side of parties where she could observe and comment.

But that was what I liked about her. She was sly and clever, and she did whatever she wanted. She didn't need anyone else. Claire was the most independent woman I had ever met. So somehow it made it all the more flattering that she wanted to spend time with me and my brothers.

After I had picked up two plates of food, I wandered over to the table where Claire and Kim sat. Claire had Kim laughing, and it seemed like she had already met a bunch of guys.

As soon as she saw me, Claire scooted over on the bench to make room. I sat down and placed her plate in front of her. "I guessed cheeseburger."

"You guessed correct," she said. "I also would have accepted hot dog, burger, or grilled mushroom."

I laughed as Claire dug into her food. Of course she wasn't a picky eater. She was too full of energy and life to waste time complaining about food.

"So," Claire said as she gave Moves a focused look. "I think I need a rundown on your role in the club, it sounds intense."

A slow smile crept across Moves' face. Anyone who didn't know him would think it was a harmless grin. But everyone who had seen Moves in action knew that smile. It was a dangerous smile. He wore it whenever he had to channel his inner violence.

Strangely enough, Claire seemed to recognize the intensity behind Moves' expression. The sunny smile did not fade from her face, but I felt her spine stiffen next to me.

"Best not to ask questions if you don't want the answers," Moves said.

"Oh, I always want the answers," Claire shot back, quick as a whip.

Moves leaned back and raised his brows. I stifled a smile. Claire wasn't going to be teased by Moves, and I liked that.

"Don't let him scare you," Kim interjected. "Moves is a big softie who only throws punches when it's for a good cause."

"Come on, Kimmy, don't ruin my rep," Moves said.

Claire laughed and turned to me.

"It's true," I said. "We all have rules that we follow, that's why our club is so strong."

"What kind of rules?" Claire asked.

"It's like this," Kim said. "When you're wearing the patch, you're not representing yourself anymore, you're representing the Outlaw Souls – so anything you do or say, that's on the brothers. That means you can't just go rogue and do whatever. You have to respect your brothers enough to stay in line."

"As opposed to illegal stuff?" Claire asked.

"We don't fuck with that."

We all turned to see Raul behind us. He was only a little bit older, in his thirties, but since he was the road captain, we all gave him the same respect we gave the old guard.

Claire picked up on that right away and nodded. "I didn't mean to offend."

"I know," he said. "And you have a right to wonder, seeing as you just got involved with Pin. So I thought I'd come out and say it, we're not that kind of club."

Claire nodded and leaned closer to me. "Good."

Raul sat down and we chatted about the gigs we did and other club news. It felt natural. Claire had questions, admitting to her ignorance of biker culture, but even so, she fit in. No one minded explaining things to her. And between Kim and Raul, she did not lack for teachers.

After Raul gave Claire an entire breakdown of Outlaw Souls' territory, I decided to save her. I grabbed her hand and pulled her around the party, introducing her to everyone else.

I kept getting the same look from my brothers. A knowing nod and maybe a wink as they smiled at Claire. It would have been embarrassing if I hadn't known that they meant well. They liked her, and they liked her with me.

It was a big deal to bring a girl to a barbecue. We didn't just bring anyone. Introducing someone you were dating to the brothers meant something.

I hadn't thought too much about it when Moves suggested I invite Claire. Instead, I had acted on instinct. If I had thought too much about the implications, then I wouldn't have asked her. It would have freaked me out that after I took this step, there was no taking it back.

I wasn't freaked. In fact, I was feeling pretty great about all my decisions.

As the sun set, we all gathered around a small fire pit and continued to chat and throw back beers. Claire sat close to me on the bench, so that I could feel her warmth through my jeans.

I couldn't help but glance down at her every few seconds, just to confirm again and again that she was real and there with me. Every time I looked at her, I noticed something else. How her cheeks flushed red after her second drink. Or how she had an extra piercing in the cartilage of her left ear. Or how she did this sharp intake of breath right before she laughed at something really funny.

As the night wore on, I tried to remember if things had

ever felt so right between me and a lady. I couldn't recall. Sara had been so long ago, and all the early memories were tainted with what had happened later. I couldn't think of her without recalling her betrayal.

But even so, I didn't think our connection had been as strong as mine with Claire. We had been teenagers, filled with hormones and lust, but that was all just physical. Not to say there was no physical aspect with Claire, there certainly was. But there was something deeper. Something I hadn't allowed myself to feel in a long time. Something I hadn't really believed existed.

I slipped away to grab another round of drinks and ran into Raul by the cooler. He gave me a head nod. As I grabbed a drink out of the ice, he opened his mouth. "Claire's a keeper."

I tried to stay nonchalant since I had been attempting to not show all my brothers how head-over-heels I was, but I was finding that act to be more and more difficult. So I smiled and nodded instead. "I get that feeling too."

"Be careful," Raul said. "She's tough as nails, but I'm guessing that's why you like her."

I stiffened at Raul's warning. Claire was tough, but she wasn't cruel. I didn't think so anyway.

"I didn't mean to butt in," Raul said. "Seems like she has a secret or two, that's all. But then again, don't we all?"

I frowned. I didn't want to doubt Claire, but my curiosity got the better of me. If I was blinded by lust, I wanted someone else to point out what I couldn't see.

"How do you know?" I asked. "That she has a secret?"

Raul shrugged. "It's in the eyes. They move too much."

I stared at the ground. Raul did have a habit of being a bit dramatic, but he was smart. I wasn't about to dismiss him.

"I'm not saying she's bad," Raul said. "Truly, I like her. I just know you don't trust easy."

"That's for sure," I said. "And thanks, I'll be careful."

Raul nodded and drifted away. I turned back to Claire. The caution that had crept into my stomach while I talked to Raul evaporated in a millisecond as she tipped her head and made some sly comment to Kim.

Maybe Claire had secrets, but so did I. We all had baggage. But for the first time in my entire life, I was ready to take someone on despite any obstacles. I was ready to let her in.

If she hadn't looked so happy, surrounded by the most important people in my life, I would have hesitated. If my brothers hadn't liked her so much and made it clear that they thought she was right for me, I would have questioned everything.

But none of that had happened. Claire seemed to appreciate and respect the Outlaw Souls, and they adored her. I could already tell that Kim was plotting more ways to hang out with Claire while I could tell that all the guys thought she was cool. I would have been jealous if I didn't know that a brother would never try and poach another Outlaw Soul's girl.

For the first time in a long time, everything was making sense. I finally felt permission to be happy. Not just happy for one night. Not just happy when I was working or riding with my brothers but lonely the rest of the time. Truly and fully happy.

There was no doubt in my mind: I was falling for Claire.

EIGHTEEN
CLAIRE

Nothing made sense. Up was down, left was right. I felt like I was Alice, and I had just tumbled down the rabbit hole or through the looking glass or whatever other mess that silly girl got into.

The Outlaw Souls were a little rough around the edges, that was true. They liked to throw back some beers and tell raunchy jokes, and, as bikers, they clearly liked a little danger. But there was no older guy dragging around a manipulated teen. There was no drug activity or even references to drugs. Not even tension among the brothers. To be honest, it was all pretty wholesome.

Yes, they had dirty mouths, a lot of them had tattoos, and I heard one of the older guys mention his time in jail, but none of that was criminal or even out of the ordinary.

I had known that I wasn't going to walk into that barbecue and find Zoe by the hot dogs, wailing about how her one-time cool and sophisticated boyfriend made her sell cocaine, but I also knew that fires give off smoke. You can't hide everything. Illicit activity leaves signs, and I was pretty good at reading those signs. I had figured that there would be at least a whiff of smoke at the party.

But there was nothing. Every instinct in my body was screaming that the brothers of the Outlaw Souls were exactly what they said they were: hardscrabble guys from the wrong side of the track who took care of each other and stuck to a strong moral code of values. If anything, they were way more Robin Hood than Al Capone.

Hell, Moves had even ran through their most recent gigs. Security for big events and helping out on construction sites. A few of the guys did a lot of auto work at a shop I knew was the most trustworthy in La Playa. The Outlaw Souls, despite their name and leathers, were upstanding pillars of the community.

Or they were very, very good liars. I couldn't deny that the possibility that they were duping me rubbed me the wrong way. I like to think that I can spot a liar.

I smiled at Pin and told him I was going to run to the restroom. I couldn't imagine we were going to stay at the party much longer since it was already pretty late, so I wanted a moment alone to take stock.

I sat in the stall of the women's restroom of Blue Dog Saloon and stared at the graffiti on the bathroom door. This case didn't make sense. If this party had all the members of the Outlaw Souls, then not one of them was an obvious choice for coercion of a minor and/or drug-dealing.

Granted, I had not shared soul-searching conversation with every single brother, but I had met most of them and observed the rest. I knew criminals can wear the appearance of goodness like a second skin, but there still would have been signs. No one even had the physical traits of a drug-addict. None of them said creepy things or even looked at me cross-eyed.

I huffed in frustration as I yanked out my notebook and started to write down every name I could remember. I would research the members of the club later. Our office didn't have access to all the files at the police department, but private investigators have ways. I could find out who had done time for what.

I tried to write fast since, if I was gone too long, Pin would come looking for me.

That was the other thorn in my side with this case. The more time I spent with Pin, the more I was inclined to believe that he didn't deserve to be used like this. I didn't want to use him. I just wanted to be with him. But that thought was way too scary to explore at the moment.

Maybe I should have stuck to the cheating husbands after all. At least I was good at that stuff. At least trailing scumbags didn't make me question my every action.

Maybe I just wasn't cut out for the big cases.

I shook my head and snapped my notebook shut. No, I could do this. I was used to catching idiots who thought with their dicks. This was just a smarter opponent. Whoever had orchestrated Zoe and Hector's fate was more complex and certainly smarter. Catching them would take more time, but it didn't mean I wasn't up to the task.

I stood up, shoved my notebook back in my bag, and walked out of the bathroom. I collided right into Pin's chest. "Oh, sorry."

He gripped my arm to steady me, and my heart melted at the feel of his hand on my body.

"No worries," he said. "I was actually just looking for you, I thought we might head out soon."

"Ok," I said. "No rush, I'm having a good time."

"Yeah," Pin said. "Me too."

The light in the bar was dim and intimate, and we were

tucked into the hallway with the bathrooms, alone and secluded. Pin was giving me major bedroom eyes, as if to say that yeah, the barbecue was fun, but he could think of better things we could do in private.

Before I could stop or remind myself that I was playing a dangerous game, I stood on my tiptoes and brushed a kiss against his lips. I couldn't help it. He had been so nice all day, always staying by my side so that I wouldn't be alone, but allowing me to be myself and ask questions. And all the other bikers had been so kind. I could see that they just wanted Pin to be happy.

Pin placed his firm hand on my lower back and pulled me closer. He leaned down and placed a row of fluttery kisses on my neck.

"Not here," he whispered in my ear. "If the guys catch me, they'll never stop giving us shit."

I chuckled and pulled away. "I can believe that."

We walked hand in hand back out to the fire pit. Only a few of the younger crowd remained. It was getting late, so everyone had drifted off. Most of the older guys had wives and kids (another thing that didn't quite add up with the Drug Ring theory).

Moves appeared at Pin's side. His easy manner and smile were gone, and I was immediately on high alert.

"Hey, I gotta run," Moves muttered.

He wasn't speaking so only Pin could hear, but he also wasn't shouting out the news. The Enforcer, I remembered. Moves was the enforcer. What needed enforcing?

"Trouble?" Pin asked.

"Just some bullets that need to be put back on their shelf," Moves said with a dark look.

I furrowed my brow and stared at the ground. What did that mean? It didn't sound good.

Moves disappeared, and I contemplated whether to say anything. I decided it was normal to ask. A normal girl would ask a guy on a second date why his friend was muttering about bullets and trouble. "What was that about?"

"Don't worry about it," Pin said.

I pursed my lips at his words, even though his tone was gentle. He wasn't shutting me out, he just didn't want me to fret. Even so, I didn't appreciate being kept in the dark.

"It's just territory issues," Pin said. "We're in charge of this side of La Playa, in a way, so we like to keep it as clean as possible."

It wasn't terribly enlightening, but I could tell it was all I was going to get. I nodded and tried to think of a different topic. I could search the news tomorrow to see if anything went down tonight.

"So do brothers usually bring second dates to this kind of thing?" I asked.

It was a genuine question. Over the course of the barbecue, it had become clear that it was pretty exclusive. Members and serious girlfriends or wives only. It was strange that Pin had invited me, but also flattering in a way.

I also wanted to try and steer the conversation towards dates in general. Maybe Pin would let it slip that a brother had shown up with a much younger – some might even guess high school age – date about six months ago. Maybe it would be a brother that Pin didn't know very well. Maybe Pin wouldn't be aware of any dirt I uncovered. A girl could dream.

"Not really," Pin said. "I guess I kinda threw you to the wolves."

"No, no," I said. "Everyone was really nice. I just get the idea that it means something to take someone to this."

"It does," Pin said.

He led me to a bench outside the main circle of people, and we sat down. The fire pit's glow barely reached us, so half of Pin's face was darkened by the shadows of night.

"Have you ever taken a date to a barbecue before?" I asked.

I didn't know why I asked. This line of inquiry wasn't getting me closer to Zoe or Hector, but I wanted to know. The way the other bikers had greeted me implied that Pin did not often, if ever, show up with a significant other. I was desperate to know why.

"No," Pin said. "You're the first."

I was silent as I took that in. I sensed that Pin had more to say, so I gave him space and waited.

"I haven't been in a serious relationship since I was fifteen," Pin said. "If you can even call a high school relationship serious."

"You can," I said. "Studies actually show that because the teenage brain is still developing, high school relationships may shape and affect us more than later ones."

"Yeah, well, I can probably attest to that," Pin said, leaning forward until his elbows rested on his knees. "She fucked me up. Actually, it wasn't just her. First, it was my parents, she was just the nail in the coffin."

"What do you mean?" I whispered.

I was desperate for more details, but I didn't want to ask too many aggressive questions and cause him to clam up. I knew how hard it was to open up about the past sometimes.

"I hate blaming my mom because I know she did her best," Pin said. "But I had to watch her fall in love with guys who screwed her over again and again. And then I went and fell for the same type of person."

I didn't even breathe as Pin stared into space; as he looked back in time.

"She cheated on me," Pin said. "Which really isn't a big deal, it happens all the time, but that just proves what I always suspected. People will usually betray you if given the chance."

My eyes widened at his bleak outlook. My heart broke for the pain lurking beneath Pin's calm and pulled-together surface.

"I'm so sorry," I said. "I guess that doesn't really make anything better, but I am."

"I just haven't wanted to even try with anyone since," Pin said. "Because why bother?"

I recognized something in his tone. Hadn't I thought the same thing to myself more times than I could count over the last few years? All my relationships ended, so why bother?

"But with you," Pin said. "I want to try again."

He looked over at me, and his expression took my breath away. It was not lost on me what this meant. This was not just a casual hook-up, nor was it even dating at this point. This was something else. Something big and terrifying and thrilling.

I hadn't intended to share too much with Pin. I had wanted to stay coy and subdued. But I couldn't just sit there after his admission. Without even realizing it, I opened my mouth.

"It's hard for me too," I said. "To try."

Pin just looked at me as I cleared my throat and tried to clear my head. Somewhere deep inside, I knew I should be focused on the case. I should deflect Pin's desire to have a heavy conversation and get back to mining his friends for information. That knowledge was buried, however, beneath a surge of emotion that surprised me with its intensity.

"My whole life, I've always wanted more," I said. "Something more exciting or different than what I had. And I'm not ashamed of the life I want."

Pin nodded, and I felt safe with him. I felt I could trust him to not judge me.

"I am ashamed by how I've come up with excuses," I said. "Every time I start to get close to someone, I get scared they're just going to hold me back or tie me down, so as soon as I'm a little bit bored, I drop them."

I clamped my mouth shut. I hadn't even known what I was going to say. I had barely been able to admit as much to myself. I knew I got bored with nearly every guy, and I knew my boredom had something to do with my fear of being held down in one place. But it was hard to come face to face with your own fears.

Somehow Pin had made it easier.

"I can't promise you much," I said. "But I can promise you that I'll try."

"Good." Pin smiled, and it was like the sun was rising on a new chapter of my life. "I promise I'll try too."

He reached over and took my hand in his. Somehow that small point of contact felt far more intimate than anything else we had done. It was physical touch with the added knowledge of each other. Perhaps it had only been for a moment, but we had each bore a part of ourselves.

Without another word, we stood up. Pin waved goodbye to the people remaining by the fire before leading me out to the front of the Blue Dog Saloon so we could wait for a car.

During the ride back to my place, we talked about the barbecue and laughed over the funny moments. By the time we reached my apartment, I didn't even pretend that he wasn't invited up. I wasn't even thinking about the case anymore. I couldn't think about it just then.

I hadn't figured anything out in regards to the Outlaw Souls involvement in any sort of illicit drug ring. All I knew was that I needed to be with Pin that night.

And that I really, really hoped he wasn't involved with anything bad.

NINETEEN
PIN

After our talk at the barbecue, I felt as if I was floating on a cloud. I had entered an alternate reality. Someplace I never thought I would gain entrance to. I wasn't supposed to find this kind of connection with someone. I was too cynical, too rough, too poor.

Yet somehow I was there with Claire.

I had been scared to tell her about my past at the barbecue, but I'd known if I didn't, I would feel like I was lying. Claire deserved to know that she was different from other women I had been involved with. She also deserved to know what she was getting into with me, so she could back out if she decided she didn't want a damaged commitment-phobe.

Only she hadn't backed out. Instead, she had met me halfway. And it only made me fall harder for her. I understood her fear of being tied down. I was determined to make sure Claire always knew that I wasn't a weight around her neck or something holding her back. I wanted her to have her freedom to chase any adventure she picked.

She was quiet as she once again let me into her apartment. As soon as we were through the door, she kicked off her black boots. They hadn't been very high heels, but she looked much smaller with them off.

She fixed me with a look that turned my insides to molten fire. The other night had been cozy and comfortable. We had been feeling out the waters, getting to know each other. This night was different. This time we wanted more from each other.

I stepped forward and pulled Claire against me like I had wanted to all night. Her torso was warm and alive under my hands. She stood on her tiptoes to kiss me, gently at first, but her mouth grew more and more urgent.

She pulled away and started to run her fingers over the light scruff on my cheeks while she plastered my neck with kisses.

"Claire," I murmured. "I've wanted you all day."

"Me too," she whispered.

I couldn't hold back. In a flash, I leaned down, put one arm beneath her knees and the other at her back, then scooped her into my arms.

Claire let out a delighted yelp. She wrapped her arms around my neck as if I had lifted her up a hundred times and continued to kiss me.

I walked over to the couch and sat down. Claire was a compelling weight upon my lap. She wiggled to get comfortable, and with each squirm, she sent lightning bolts of desire coursing through me.

I held her as tight as I could against my chest and kissed her soft lips. I started by flicking my tongue along her lower lip and then gradually thrust my tongue deeper into her mouth. Claire responded like clay, her petal-soft skin turning pink and flushed.

I willed myself to focus on the feel of her in my arms. I wanted to remember all the details with clarity, so I could take this memory out later and relive it. I was obsessed with how her body was simultaneously firm and soft. She had muscles lining her arms, back and abs, but nothing bulging with her every muscle coated in a delightful layer of tender flesh.

I could tell she was lithe and strong, but it was almost as if her body was spun out of a finer material than mine. The very fibers of her being were more complex and delicate.

Her hand suddenly fluttered across my chest as she moved her fingers to the button on her dress. The hem of her skirt was already hitched up around her thighs as I grasped her hands, stopping her from continuing to undress. I held her wrists with one hand and reached for her collar with my other.

"Let me," I said. "I want to take my time, if that's alright?"

Claire nodded as if in a daze. "Yes. I want that too."

I unbuttoned her dress, but paused between each button to kiss her mouth or cheeks or neck. Claire sighed with pleasure and ran her own hands up and down my shoulders. I pulled her dress aside to reveal inch by inch of her creamy skin. The buttons ran all the way down her outfit, so soon the entire front was open. Claire's pert breasts were encased in a lacy black bra with the silvery-white of her stomach exposed.

I leaned back against the couch so I could take her in. I wanted to remember the sight of her in addition to the feel of her body.

Claire didn't let me look for long. She snuck her hands beneath my cotton T-shirt and ran searching fingers over my torso before lifting the clothing over my head. Once the shirt was discarded, she leaned over and started licking and nipping at my chest. I sucked in my breath and let her have her fun. I wanted us to explore each other. I wanted us to delight in one another.

I hissed in pleasure as Claire adjusted her legs so that she was straddling me. Now she was pressed up against my erection, and I liked knowing that she could feel how much she turned me on. I could feel the warmth of her as well, and I couldn't resist slipping a finger beneath the hem of her panties.

I ran a teasing touch along the top of her thatch of curls before sliding it lower and just lightly touching her sensitive clitoris. I was rewarded by Claire whimpering in response and kissing me with renewed fervor.

She pressed herself against my hand with an eagerness that made me want to rush to the finish line. Something about her made me feel like a teenager again, desperate to hurry through sex to reach my satisfaction. I took a breath and regained control.

I could tell she wanted me to touch her more down there, so instead, I teased her by running my hands everywhere else on her body. I kneaded her ass and felt her shiver as I ran my hand up her side. Then I slipped my hand beneath one bra and cupped her breast. I pinched her nipple between two fingers until I felt it harden.

Claire was making little mewling sounds of pleasure with every move I made, and it was the hottest thing in the world. She tugged a strap of her bra over one shoulder so that her nipple was exposed. Without hesitating, I took the hard nipple in my mouth and began sucking her. She dug her fingers into my shoulders and began moving her hips against mine.

The motion drove me crazy with desire. I had never been so hard, my entire cock burned with a need to be inside her. Soon. Soon, I would be satisfied, but I wanted to take Claire to the brink first.

Without pausing in my attention to her breast, I slipped my hand back underneath her panty, but this time I wasn't as timid. I ran my fingers across her folds, just feeling how wet she was for me made my erection throb. I began to tease and touch her clitoris, making Claire move atop my hand with increasing urgency.

"That feels so good, Pin," she murmured. "Oh, it feels so good."

I was about to take things further when all of a sudden, Claire leaned back and vacated my lap. I gasped at how cold I felt without her, and I blinked in concern that I had done something wrong.

"What?" Before I could finish my question, I realized what Claire was doing. She had kneeled between my legs, her dress still half on, and her fingers prying at the zipper of my jeans.

"No, Claire," I said. "You don't have to."

"I want to," Claire said, tugging my pants down to reveal the evidence of my own desires. "I want to make you feel good."

Then she raised one playful brow and leaned closer, her mouth a pink little O above the tip of my erection. "But if you don't *want* me to continue, I'll stop."

A smile tugged at my lips. I adored that she was so playful in bed. I should have known she would be up to wrestle the control from me. I liked it. It made us feel like equals.

Before I could dwell anymore on how much I appreciated Claire, she took me in her mouth, and I lost all powers of rational thought. She licked and sucked and massaged me with her hand, all while giving me the most sensual look with her big blue eyes.

"Oh God." I leaned back with a cry. "Oh *God*."

When Claire had driven me almost to the edge, I knew I needed to stop her. I loved what she was doing, but I didn't want to come yet. Not until she was fully satisfied. I sat up and Claire raised her head. Before she could ask me what was going on, I pulled her against my chest and was rising from the couch.

She squealed once again as I carried her to the bedroom. I sat her on the bed and just stood in front of her for a moment, taking her in from her tousled blonde hair to her swollen lips to her little feet, dangling above the floor.

Then I stepped forward and pushed the dress off her. I disposed of her bra and panties in quick succession. Claire had already tugged my pants down, and I removed my boxer shorts, so that we were both naked, totally exposed to each other.

I approached the bed and she squirmed back until I was propped horizontally on my elbows while she was beneath me. I kissed her slowly and passionately, relishing the feel of her hands on my back that pulled me closer.

Then I began to touch her again, flicking and massaging her clitoris until she was whimpering with sensation. When I knew she couldn't take it anymore, I slid one finger inside her. The feel of her warm, tight pussy was enough to almost make me come early.

I clenched my teeth and bit her lip before growling in her ear. "Claire, I want to be inside you."

"I want that too," Claire gasped. "Please, Pin."

I wanted her a million different ways. I wanted her from behind on her hands and knees. I wanted her on top and I wanted her on bottom. I wanted to make love to her on the beach, in a car, on the floor, wherever. I wanted to do everything with her.

But for now, I knew I could only hold onto my self-control for so long. Claire was on the brink of losing control as well.

So I slid into her and cried out as I realized that my memory from last time hadn't even done her justice. She felt even better than I remembered. The warmth of her clenching around me was even more satisfying than I had imagined. And I had been doing a lot of imagining.

I thrust into her again and again, and in answer, Claire wrapped her legs around my waist to pull me closer. She matched my rhythm as I reached down to work her clitoris with my fingers, eliciting little screams from Claire's mouth.

I expected her to close her eyes as the waves of her orgasm started to build, but instead, she kept her eyes wide open and fixed upon me. I held her gaze and watched with joy as her eyes widened as her climax began to grow.

"Oh, Pin," she cried. "Pin!"

I thrust even harder and she went flying over the edge, her pussy flexing around me as the courses of pleasure took her. I exploded only a moment after, letting out a primal yell as my own body was overtaken with a wave of ecstasy.

As our cries mingled between us, the whole room faded into a blur. All I could see was the blue of Claire's eyes, and all I could feel was the slickness of her dewy skin.

When we had both exhausted the final jolts of our climaxes, I tumbled onto my back beside her. In a heartbeat, Claire had hitched one leg over my thigh and put her head on my chest.

"Is this ok?" she asked.

I drew her closer with my arm. Serenity descended on me like a heated comforter. "Of course."

"It's just last time you left," Claire said.

She wasn't whining or accusing. She just wanted to know where we stood. She was confirming that things had changed.

"I'm not going to leave tonight." I wasn't going to even let go of her for many hours.

First of all, because I fully intended to fuck her again, once we had both recovered. I was already dreaming up new positions.

Second, I knew it was going to be hard to sleep away from her, this night and in the future. I had gotten a taste of what it felt like to be with her sexually. I knew how it felt for her to sleep curled up against me. I was already addicted to her.

Claire let out a little sigh of contentment and nestled her head even closer to my neck.

"But if you sleep naked like this, you do know I won't be able to resist, right?" I asked.

Claire placed one hand on my lower stomach, dangerously close to my crotch. "Oh, I'm counting on it."

With a grin, I reached up to lift her chin, and I kissed her, once more. I was never going to be able to stop kissing her. I couldn't stop touching her.

And the most shocking part: I didn't even want to try and stop.

TWENTY

CLAIRE

I don't often admit to making mistakes, but that's because I don't often mess up. When I do commit an error, though, I like to think I can own up to it.

I was positive I had made a mistake with Pin. I had thought I could use him for the case and then discard him. I had thought my attraction was run-of-the-mill lust, easily forgotten in a week or so.

I was wrong. I was not going to forget this night any time soon.

I couldn't say when things had gotten more intense, but they had. Somewhere between the Chinese food and the barbecue, our relationship had taken a turn. It had gone from light and casual, no strings attached, to something far heavier.

It was strange though, I didn't feel oppressed by the weight. In the past, when boyfriends made serious confessions or declared their emotions, I always felt burdened, as if now I had to lug around the weight of their feelings in a back around my neck.

I didn't feel that way with Pin. I felt safe with his

emotions. I was touched that he cared about me to break his old habits, and I found that I wanted to do the same for him.

It didn't hurt that he was amazing in bed. His every touch sent flames of want rippling across my body. Even now, laying against him in the post-sex cuddling position, I was already wondering when he would be up for another round.

Before I could give in to drowning myself in the feeling of being with him, I rolled onto my back. He was dozing a bit, but he kept his solid arm across my torso. I had to think a few things through. The twinge of guilt I felt before the barbecue over using Pin had grown into a growling beast, clawing at the lining of my stomach.

I stared at the ceiling and asked myself if it was time to come clean. To my surprise, the answer was a definitive yes. There was no other option. I could not continue to lie to him. I cared about him too much.

Besides, he had been totally honest with me tonight. I had responded with some honesty, but not total honesty. I wanted to actually match him. I wanted to tell the truth. But how would he react?

I glanced over at him, my breath catching at the way his dark eyelashes brushed his cheeks with shadowy kisses. I didn't want to lose him. I wanted him to come back and share my bed and take me on more rides. I wouldn't get bored of him, and I would never hurt him.

Or I would never hurt him any more than I already had.

It was a frightening realization that I might not make it out of this with him. He might walk away and not return. It had taken a lot for him to let down his walls with me. I could tell when he was explaining his distrust of relationships.

I wanted to defend myself. I wanted to say that I hadn't

cheated on him. I would never do that. I had only lied to him. Just a little. Not even a lie really. I had just hung out with him in the hopes to uncover a drug ring within his beloved biker club.

Squeezed my eyes shut, I wondered if that was that worse than cheating? Possibly. I guess it didn't matter which was worse. What mattered was that I had done it.

As I heaved a sigh, Pin stirred beside me and inched his hand up towards my breast. I turned to him and he kissed me, his eyes blinking out of their slumber. I melted into the kiss, and soon we were wrapped together again to the point I couldn't tell where I ended and he began.

He touched me again, gently easing me back into the land of pleasure, where I couldn't think about my sins. Where I could only feel his hands and lips on me.

It didn't take us long to reach a frantic state of desire once again. This time I climbed atop him and lowered myself onto his erection, savoring the fullness I felt as I took him as deep as I could. I gazed down at his body as his hands gripped my hips, and we found a rhythm. I gasped as my orgasm consumed me. He convulsed and cried out, letting me know that he was in the same state.

When we were done, I held him inside for a bit longer and lay down across his chest. He wrapped his arms around me, and I wanted to be held by him forever.

I rolled off and onto my side, but Pin pulled my back against his chest so he was spooning me. I closed my eyes, and tears trickled out. I let them roll in silence down my cheek. If Pin knew I was crying, he would hold me and comfort me and ask me to tell him what was wrong.

I couldn't tell him right then, but I knew I had to tell him. I would tell him, once I let him sleep. Pin deserved a restful night. He had done nothing wrong.

Tomorrow, I told myself.

Tomorrow I will tell him, and try and explain it right. I would tell him that it was my job and I got assigned this case. I would admit that it had been wrong of me to text him to hang out just so I could gain access to the Outlaw Souls.

But I would also explain that I no longer suspected that the Outlaw Souls were involved. I had observed them, and I couldn't fathom any one of those bikers seducing and manipulating a teenage girl or badgering a young teen boy into dealing drugs.

In fact, I could use Pin's help with the case. If the Outlaw Souls weren't the culprits, who were? Pin knew La Playa, he knew bikers, and he knew about the seedy side of the city. If I came clean and asked him for his help, he could be my biggest asset. He could break the case wide open.

Most importantly, I had to let Pin know that our connection was real. I hadn't been faking anything. Even when we were just hanging out watching TV, I had been myself. I had just been trying to find extra information.

As for the barbecue and everything after, I hadn't even been thinking about the case. I had just been falling for him. I just had to make him understand that, and maybe he wouldn't drop me cold turkey. It wasn't going to be an easy conversation, but I knew I had to try.

Things felt different with Pin. I no longer feared growing bored, but it wasn't just because he was a biker and that boredom wasn't part of his type or lifestyle. It was more than that. It was this strange knowledge that I could wake up morning after morning and just do the little things with Pin but not feel scared or annoyed. Pin wasn't going to hold me back from adventure. He was an adventure. Loving him could be an amazing adventure.

I shivered to myself. I hadn't dared to think the word

"love" – not yet. It came so quickly to mind though, while in Pin's arms. I took a breath to steady myself. I could consider the love question later. After I told Pin the truth.

I lay awake for a long time. I couldn't fall asleep, and I didn't really want to. I wanted the night to last forever. I wanted to stay frozen in this moment when I knew how much Pin cared for me. He thought I was wonderful and smart and beautiful. He didn't know I was a sneak. He didn't know I had suspected his family of doing horrible things. That I had gone to that barbecue like a snake in the grass.

I stopped the self-flagellation after a while. I've never been the type to beat myself up. I reminded myself that I had just been doing my job. That lives were at risk. I hadn't even known Pin that well when I accepted the assignment, and I would've been an idiot if I didn't ask questions about Outlaw Souls when I knew two teenagers had gone missing after being linked to a local biker club.

Pin might be hurt, but he wasn't stupid. He would listen to my side of the story. It could all work out. I wasn't enough of a blind optimist to think it was definitely going to be ok, but I allowed for the possibility that we could move past this.

Tomorrow, I will tell him.

Tonight I would hang onto the possibility that he would forgive me.

TWENTY-ONE
PIN

The sun streaking through the window woke me up, but had no effect on Claire. I grinned at the sight of her, out cold underneath the covers. It was what I had been hoping for. To make up for the time I had tip-toed out in the dead of night, I was going to let her sleep in while I cooked breakfast.

I knew my way around the kitchen because of the last time. As I took out a pan and some eggs, I decided that Claire should see my place too. I liked my privacy, but I didn't want to be the type of guy who always showed up at the girl's place and never allowed her into his space.

It was nice to imagine Claire curled up in my bed sheets or surveying my fridge's contents. I would give her a drawer in my dresser so she could put some spare clothes, and maybe even some space in my bathroom cabinet.

It was foreign, this practice of thinking ahead. I had never considered stuff like making room for someone in my own apartment, and I had certainly never contemplated how a relationship would progress over time.

I had always thought people who thought like that were

stupid. Relationships couldn't grow or progress, they could only deteriorate. At best, I figured relationships might grow for a while, but then they inevitably hit a plateau that was so difficult and infuriating that someone eventually took a stick of dynamite and blew up the entire thing.

It was early days, I had to admit, but I couldn't imagine Claire and I hitting a plateau. She was too full of life and too eager for adventure to ever get boring. And if things were difficult, I knew Claire well enough to know she would speak up. She would always tell it to me straight, and I would always be honest with her.

I wasn't so far gone to consider myself an expert on relationships, but I figured if we started with honesty and kindness, that was a good thing.

I cracked a few eggs into a bowl and started to laugh to myself as I began to whisk them. How had I gone from the biggest anti-romantic on the West Coast to daydreaming about my perfect relationship, all while cooking breakfast for a woman?

It was Claire, plain and simple. She was unlike anyone I had ever met. I couldn't quite describe it, but it was the way she seemed to be in constant motion. Raul had said her eyes moved fast, and he was right. But it was only because she was so eager to consume life. She wanted to see everything, meet everyone and take it all into her whirring mind.

The rest of her body moved fast as well, now that I thought about it. I had never seen Claire dilly-dally or walk slow. She moved from point A to point B with speed and a self-assured stride. That was probably why she enjoyed riding my bike so much. She relished in getting places fast.

I put the eggs on heat, and then moved to the coffee machine. I didn't drink much coffee, but I knew Claire downed it like crazy. It probably contributed to her boundless energy. It wasn't just her energy that drew me to her though.

There was something about her that matched me. I might not have realized it at first, or maybe I only recognized it subconsciously, but she understood me. She also had struggled with commitment and trusting that any relationship could be successful for the long-term. I knew she understood as soon as she explained her own past at the barbecue.

It was cheesy, but that kind of stuff must be what people mean when they talk about "soulmates" and all that other shit. Or at least, I used to think it was bullshit. Now everything had shifted. With the right person, I didn't have to feel fear. History didn't have to repeat itself. I wasn't going to walk in and find Claire in someone else's arms. It was true, she might hurt me in other ways, but she wasn't the type of person to cheat. She wasn't like that.

I would never cheat on her, and I would do everything I could to avoid hurting her. There was risk, of course. I knew there was always a risk, I hadn't lost all my powers of reason and logic. I just now understood that the reward was worth the risk.

I was grateful for my mother and Sara, in a twisted sort of way. If they hadn't shown me all the ways a relationship could get fucked up, if they hadn't made me wary of committing, I might not have found Claire. I might have jumped into some lesser relationship and not been at the Blue Dog Saloon on that fateful night.

Now I was musing about things like fate and destiny. This truly was a bizarre turn of events. I didn't care though. I was happy.

I remembered something my mother had once said to me, back after I watched the fourth or fifth guy leave her high and dry. I was a bit older then, almost out of high school, and I had started talking back to her.

She was sulking in the kitchen, downing a bottle of cheap wine and calling the guy over and over, leaving weepy voicemails. I could hear the spiraling through my bedroom wall. At last, I stormed into the kitchen.

"He's not coming back," I said. "Just like the last one, and the one before that."

My mother didn't even argue or respond. She just stared ahead in miserable silence.

"You're weak," I told her. "And you keep making the same mistakes – when will you learn your lesson?"

As soon as I said it, I felt bad. The anger trickled out of me, and I deflated. I didn't apologize though. Everything I had said was true.

After a few moments of silence, when I was about to turn around and leave my mother to her agony, she spoke.

"You'll understand someday," she said. "You'll understand when you meet someone who makes the very ground shift beneath your feet. After that, the whole world is different."

I scoffed and returned to my room. I didn't want to hear any more about whatever sappy movie my mother had gotten that line out of.

That was after Sara, and she certainly had not changed my worldview. Nothing earth-shaking about her, except for how she proved that love couldn't be trusted. I doubted my mother even meant what she said. She couldn't possibly want me to end up like her.

Now, as I finished the scrambled eggs for Claire, I thought I might see what my mother had been trying to say. It wasn't just love or lust or even respect. There was something else with Claire, a way she seemed to make everything a brighter color when she was around. When I was with her, I saw an entirely different future for myself, and I liked it far better than anything else I had seen.

Quite simply, Claire had changed my worldview. The ground had moved, but it wasn't caving in. There was no avalanche. It had shifted before I even realized it and resettled, and now I found myself on better footing. The earth was solid beneath me, but I could see everything better from my new vantage point.

There was an overwhelming urge to swing by to see my mom today. I wasn't about to say that I was wrong about everything, or that she had made amazing decisions, but I was willing to at least sympathize with where she had been coming from. She must have experienced something like what I had with Claire at least once, and she had longed for it so much that she kept trying to get that feeling back.

Now that I knew what it was like to have someone who made you hope for a better life, I could see why she had rushed into relationships so fast. I didn't know if I would be able to say all that, but I could at least smile at her. Ask how she was doing. Maybe even introduce her to Claire.

My mom would love to hear PI stories from Claire – she adored reality TV and soap operas. Claire would be happy to regale her with some drama-filled anecdotes. We could even have dinner together, just us three. It would be the first quality time I had spent with my mother in a long while.

With the eggs done, I set to work on a few strips of bacon. While they cooked, I grabbed plates and utensils. I had to open and close a few cabinets before I found the right one. I felt a little bad touching Claire's things without her there. Obviously, there was nothing scandalous in her kitchen, but I didn't want to be a snoop.

It had been so long since I had spent any non-bedroom

time in a woman's apartment. I was unused to the rituals. But I could adapt. Claire and I would figure it out, one step at a time.

I put the eggs and bacon onto a plate, poured the coffee into a mug, and took a second to marvel at my handiwork. Who knew I would prove so good at love and relationships?

I froze, my hand holding the coffee pot suspended in mid-air. Was it love? Was I ready to call it that? I couldn't say for certain. I knew I cared about Claire more than anyone I had ever met. I knew I wanted to try with her. Like I had told her at the barbecue, I wanted to attempt to find the real deal. The whole shebang.

I hadn't said those words lightly. I hadn't meant that I wanted to date seriously for a few months or years. I meant forever. What was the point of trying if it wasn't forever?

Claire had understood that, I was certain. Even so, I didn't know if I was ready to say love. That was another heavy word, one I might save for a later day. I was on my way there, though, that was for certain. And I was definitely in the fast lane.

Not today, but someday, I would tell her.

The thought didn't terrify me. In fact, it made me smile.

I left the food on the counter and moved to clear her small kitchen table. I was excited to wake her up and watch her guzzle her coffee and just talk with her a bit.

I pushed a few books and newspapers to one side of the table and grabbed her big purse from a chair. I just planned to move it to the couch really quickly, but it was placed sideways on the chair. When I picked it up, a dark green notebook fell to the floor.

We had been in a rush last night, so Claire must not have been paying too much attention to where she placed her purse, I thought with a grin. I tossed the purse on the couch before bending down to scoop up the notebook. I had seen it on Claire before and I figured it must be her journal or day planner.

It was private, that was for sure, and I had no intention of snooping through it.

But it fell face down on the floor, with its cover open and pages splayed out. So that when I picked it up, I did see the top of one page. I just saw two words, but they were enough to make me stop in my tracks as my blood ran cold.

Outlaw Souls.

Those were the two words written in big letters across the top of one page. I held the book and looked straight ahead. I didn't want to read it. I knew in that moment, reading whatever was in that book was not going to make me feel good. Yes, Claire could have just been writing a diary entry about me and biker clubs. Or she could have been penciling the barbecue into her schedule. There were plenty of innocent explanations.

But when I saw those letters, written in such a neat and purposeful hand (every letter clearly defined), I knew there was no easy explanation. That wasn't Claire. Whatever was in this notebook, it wasn't innocent or simple. The back of my neck prickled with apprehension.

I knew the notebook held nothing good, and yet I had to read it. I couldn't just set it aside. Those were my people. My family. If Claire was writing about them in her notebook, I had to see for myself what she was saying.

I could ask Claire about it, but I would never know if whatever she told me was the truth. And I had to know. There was no way forward if I didn't know.

Slowly, I turned the book in my hands and looked down. Claire had perfect handwriting. I don't know why I fixated on that first, but she did. Every letter was formed with total preciseness. It made reading her notes easy.

In a matter of seconds, I had my answers. I skimmed a few pages, then flipped back and read a few more pages with more care. An investigation.

Claire was investigating the Outlaw Souls.

She actually thought we were dealing drugs and stealing underaged girls and boys away from their families. She had met my brothers, shared food and laughed with them, but the whole time she was taking notes on them. The whole time, she was able to look them in the eyes while she suspected them of horrible things.

And me. I was selfish enough that I wasn't just furious about her suspicions of Outlaw Souls. I was angrier about how she had used me. Sleeping with me that first night after the club, inviting me over to eat takeout, going to the barbecue with me. And last night.

It had all been an act. Her every move was orchestrated to wind me around her little finger. She had wanted me to let my guard down so she could start to pry. And I had been too stupid to see any of it. Claire wasn't just naturally curious about the club, she had asked specific questions to help her fish for details about our lifestyle and income. She probably hadn't even enjoyed the bike ride, she had just pretended to so I would invite her into my life a little bit more.

Everything had been a deception. Every touch, every kiss, perhaps even her moans of passion.

I had laid my heart bare for her. I had told her things I had never told anyone. The story she recited back was probably fabricated in the moment. And I had drank it up. Believed every word.

I was an idiot. Despite everything I had seen in my life,

despite the fact that I of all people should have known better, I fell for her act hook, line and sinker.

I knew I should rage. I should want to throw the book across the room and start tearing her apartment apart. I knew I should scream at her until she woke up. But for the first few seconds, as everything settled in, I felt nothing. My heart was utterly iced over. My mind was moving fast, but my emotions had paused.

The ground had not shifted, but everything else was crumbling down around me.

I heard rustling from the bedroom behind me, and then the sound of Claire's footfalls. I turned and saw her in the doorway, and that's when the anger began to rise.

TWENTY-TWO
CLAIRE

I swung my legs over the bed and reached my arms above my head for a satisfying stretch.

Once I had fallen asleep, it had been a long and dreamless slumber. I smiled as I glanced at the indent where Pin had lain. I had heard him in the kitchen as I drifted in and out of sleep, but it was quiet now, so I figured it was time to eat.

I still knew I had to tell him the truth about the investigation today, but somehow the morning made everything seem a bit better. With the sun shining, and the smell of coffee wafting through the air, I was feeling more optimistic.

In the dark of night, it had been easy to think my mistakes might cost me Pin. But in the morning, I had more confidence in my ability to tell the story in a way that made him understand.

As for convincing him that my feelings for him were real, that had to be possible. They were real. My feelings had never been so strong for anyone, he had to see the truth in that at least. With breakfast in my stomach and some coffee in my hand, I could do this.

I slipped off my bed and grabbed a baggy white t-shirt from my dresser drawer. I pulled on some underwear and splashed some water on my face. I smiled at my reflection. I had never been fussy about hair and makeup to begin with, and I also knew that Pin didn't care. He liked me as I was. The sexiness of that nearly took my breath away.

I popped out of the bathroom and headed towards my bedroom door. I was about to call out a greeting when I saw him.

He was standing stock-still in the middle of my living room, his back turned from me.

In his hands was my notebook. My dark green notebook with all the details of the current case. It was open, and he was reading it.

I couldn't breathe. I couldn't talk. I could only stare in horror as he turned. If I had hoped that maybe he hadn't read that much or didn't understand, that hope vanished when I saw his expression.

A million emotions rippled across his face. Hurt and pain and shock. But most of all fury. He had a right to that. He had a right to feel anger.

"Pin," I gasped. "It's not what you think."

His eyes hardened, and I didn't dare go nearer. I knew Pin would never strike me, no matter how livid he was, but I also didn't want to make him storm out. I wanted to explain. It was happening all wrong, but I could still explain.

"So it's not a notebook about how you think the Outlaw Souls have kidnapped *children* and are using them to deal drugs," Pin said.

His voice was low and lethal. I had never heard him sound so flat and cold.

"It's an investigation," I said.

I wanted to cry, and I could feel my lower lip trembling,

but I held it steady. I was made of stronger stuff than that. I could stay tough through this.

"Those teens are missing, and Outlaw Souls were the main suspects when the case was assigned," I said.

"Oh, I see," Pin said. "And lucky it got assigned to a whore like you who had zero problems fucking me until I gave you the answers you wanted."

"Don't call me that!" I shouted.

"Why?" Pin asked. "It's what you are."

It infuriated me how he kept his voice so quiet when all I could do was nearly scream. My own anger began to boil in my stomach.

"I am *not* a whore," I cried. "And I didn't mean for things to happen the way they did, I promise, just let me explain."

"No," Pin said. "You don't get to explain – how am I supposed to believe a word that comes out of your fucking mouth?"

Now he was raising his voice. His fury was overriding his control, and he was pointing at me with one angry hand while he still gripped the notebook in his other.

"I know now that the Outlaw Souls didn't do anything," I said. "But a few days ago, I didn't. I had to follow the lead I was given."

Pin turned and slammed the notebook down on the table.

"You did *not* have to text me," Pin said. "You did not have to lie to me over and over – you're just telling yourself you had no choice because that's what people like you do, you step on everyone to get what you want, and then say you were just doing what you had to."

I hated how his words sounded true. He was wrong

about me. I hadn't slept with him for my job. But some of his sentences still rang true.

"I wasn't faking my feelings," I said. "You have to believe me."

"Fuck you, Claire," Pin said. "I don't have to believe a thing you say."

I recoiled from him as if he had hit me. It almost felt like he had, his words landing like missiles on my face. A lump rose in my throat. I didn't want to cry in front of him, not while he was yelling at me like this. He couldn't see my tears.

I swallowed the lump and surged forward.

"Fuck you!" I screamed. "Kids are missing, Pin, and I have to find them. I don't care if you're too self-centered to listen."

"We didn't take anyone!" Pin shouted. "We would never, we're not Las Balas! We have a code, and if you weren't such a shitty PI, you would have realized that in a matter of seconds!"

I saw red. He could insult my values. He could say horrible things about me as a person, but he could not insult my ability to do my job.

"Only an idiot wouldn't have looked into Outlaw Souls," I said. "Bikers were all over this case, and I'm sorry that I used you, that things got out of hand, but I had to do it."

I crossed my arms and willed a mask of strength to fall over my face. We couldn't have a real conversation about my feelings. Not when Pin was like this. And he might always be like this.

It was over. I had waited too long, and I had messed up everything. Now all I could do was hold onto my dignity.

"That's what you call what happened with us?" Pin asked, eyes widening. "It just *got out of hand?*"

I flinched. It wasn't what I had meant to say, but I mentally injected steel into my spine. I would not back down from him. I put a tight leash on my emotions.

"You won't listen to me, so I don't have to explain myself," I said. "I already told you I didn't fake things with you and last night was real."

"Don't fucking talk about last night," Pin said.

He turned around and gripped the table. I stood still as he took several deep breaths. When he turned around, it seemed as if he had calmed down. He had shoved all his pain into some deep corner. I felt awful that I had been the cause of this. I had hurt him so badly that he was lashing out, like a wounded animal.

After he had been so hesitant to trust anyone. After he had feared how anyone who got close would betray him. I did feel bad. But I was angry at him too. He wasn't even trying to see my side.

"I just got hired for a job," I said. "They told me to look into Outlaw Souls, and I did it. It's not personal."

I regretted the last sentence as soon as it left my mouth.

First of all, it was a lie. The case had gotten personal almost the second I had heard about it. I hated that I was lying to him again, even after he had accused me of being a liar, and I had denied it.

"You're a cold-hearted bitch," Pin said. "You really are."

My heart shattered in two. But I couldn't show it. What right did I have to a broken heart? I was the villain here. The bitch. The whore. The heartless slut.

I blinked rapidly and pressed my lips. "Get out of my apartment."

Pin stepped back and opened his mouth. He probably

had more to say. More cruel things to yell at me or more horrible names. I didn't care. I wanted him to leave. I couldn't draw this whole ordeal out any longer.

"Stop looking into Outlaw Souls," Pin said. "Don't even come near us."

I scoffed and rolled my eyes. I had just lost him, I wasn't going to give up my job as well. "You know I have to continue with this case."

"No, you don't," Pin said. "And we have *nothing* to do with those missing kids."

"That may be true," I said. "But I have to keep looking."

For a second, I thought he was going to yell again. I braced myself for his shouting. Instead, he turned on his heel and stomped over to the couch. I stood stock-still as he grabbed his jacket and boots. He didn't even put his shoes on. He just headed for the door, as if he couldn't stand one more second in my presence.

I looked away as he slammed my door shut behind him. I didn't want to see him leave. I was going to have to live the rest of my life with this memory, and it was already bad enough.

As soon as he was gone, my legs gave out. I crumbled onto the floor and clutched my knees to my chest as great heaving sobs erupted from my chest. All the tears I had held in came pouring down my face. I hadn't cried this hard for as long as I could remember, if ever.

Maybe I had cried like this when I was little and fell off my bike, but I couldn't remember it being this painful. This was a level of hurt I'd never known before. Because my heart was being ripped out of my chest. The beautiful future I had dared to dream of was crumbling before my own eyes, and it was all my fault.

That was the worst part. If someone else had been to

blame, if Pin had done something wrong, and I had ended up losing him, I would still cry. But it wouldn't be as horrible. I could still point my finger at someone else and plot revenge on someone else.

But how was I supposed to get revenge on myself?

I knew the answer as soon as I posed the question. Living with the mistakes I had made, living my life without Pin, always wondering what could have been, was going to be punishment enough. I had told lies before. I had always justified them. They were for the greater good, or lies of politeness, or even for survival. Nothing bad had ever happened, so I just kept lying. I carried deception around with me like a shield and weapon all in one.

Now it has all caught up to me. Every little white lie, every day I had spent pretending to be someone other than who I was, I was paying for all that now.

I sat on the floor of my apartment for almost an hour, as tears poured down my face in an unpausing river. I gasped for breath and blew my nose in my shirt and patted my face dry, but the tears just kept coming.

At one point, I thought I heard footsteps in the hall. I thought he was coming back, maybe to listen, maybe to tell me that he knew I had messed up, but he believed me that I hadn't been faking my feelings.

But it was all in my head. He wasn't coming back. After I realized that, I cried even harder.

He was never going to believe that the night before had been anything but a twisted manipulation. He was never going to see that I hadn't been making a desperate play for information. And on top of using him, I had insulted the one thing he cared about above all else, the Outlaw Souls.

I cried, and I cried. Three times I told myself to pull it

together. To get off the floor and keep moving. Shit happened. Life went on. Each time, I just curled up into a smaller ball and wept out a fresh batch of tears.

When my back and bottom started to hurt, I lay down on my side. I relished the hardness of my wooden floor against my cheek and side. I didn't deserve softness. I wasn't worthy of a bed. I certainly hadn't been worthy of Pin's bed. He had been everything I could possibly want. He had been funny and cool and smart and kind-hearted. He was an accountant, which was just perfect and endearing in every way.

He had been so good at being with me. He had understood me when I told him what I wanted out of life. He had laughed at my jokes and made me laugh in return. He had admired my career. He definitely did not anymore, but in the beginning he had thought my job was amazing. He had shown me how much he liked me. He had taken me to that barbecue and invited me into his inner sanctuary, unaware that I entered bearing matches and kerosene.

He had even made me breakfast, and it was sitting right there on the counter, taunting me with its scent. I had fallen in love with him. That was the truth I had to face as I lay there sobbing on my floor.

I had found something that some people spend a lifetime searching for, but I had been too stupid to even realize my luck until it was too late. I could have owned up to everything earlier. I could have told Pin about the investigation after he spent a night on my couch. I could have told him before the barbecue, or even after. He would have listened.

But I had waited and convinced myself that was for the best.

I cried, and I cried, and I knew that this wasn't like the time I fell off my bike as a child. Those scrapes and bruises had healed with time. The pain had faded. That wasn't going to happen now. Time was not going to make this better.

This was never, ever going to stop hurting.

TWENTY-THREE
PIN

I couldn't stop replaying the scene with Claire in my head.

Even as I raced along the highway on my bike, when I should have been focusing on the road, I kept seeing her face. I kept hearing her telling me to listen, telling me that she had no choice. The roar of my engine couldn't drown out how stiff and cold she had sounded when she told me to leave.

I didn't regret anything I had said. She had lied to me, and it hurt me to think of how the whole time I was worshipping her in bed, she had an ulterior moment. She had probably been wondering how to leverage our new level of intimacy.

I didn't know where I was headed. Just away. If I stayed in La Playa, I would go back to her. I would yell at her some more or beg her to explain, and I didn't know which was worse.

I had turned back as soon as I exited the apartment building. I had stood near the mailboxes for way too long, and then climbed back up the stairs. I had made it all the way to her door.

And then I heard.

Horrible gut-wrenching sobs came from within. Every bone in my body longed to break down that door and go to her. Even though I knew better, I had cared for her and those feelings wouldn't evaporate. Every instinct I had longed to comfort Claire if she was in pain. I wanted to hold her and rock her while she cried into my chest.

But that wouldn't be right. Because she wasn't mine, and she had never been mine. I didn't owe her my protection and comfort. She had shown me no respect and had trampled over my heart in her black combat boots. If I went into that apartment just because she was crying, I was saying that I was ok with what she had done.

Besides, she was probably crying because her so-called lead in the case was ruined. She wasn't sorry about what she had done, that was clear. She was only sorry she got caught. The truth was, I didn't really know her. I had fallen for an illusion. Had been enamored with a lie. The Claire I knew didn't even exist. I wanted to comfort a ghost.

So I had turned and ran out of that building as fast as I could. I had gotten a car back to my place and hopped on my bike, without even going into my apartment. I just needed to ride. A long fast ride always cleared my head. It had to work this time because I was going to need it.

My personal wounds inflicted by Claire was one thing, but the implications for Outlaw Souls were also a serious matter. We were suspects in an ongoing investigation. Claire hadn't come up with Outlaw Souls on her own. I had seen her notes about parents and police and random teenagers. Other people had pointed their fingers at us. Claire was an idiot for believing them, but she had not made the first accusation.

Which meant that we needed to have a meeting as soon

as possible. We needed to discuss why we were taking the blame for drug-dealing and child-snatching, and we needed to figure out who was at fault. We needed to solve the problem.

That's why I had asked Claire to stop investigating. She needed to get out of the way. This was biker business, plain and simple. I couldn't be distracted by her running around, hurling accusations willy-nilly and asking questions.

It had been stupid to ask her to stop. I may not have known the real Claire, but I did know she was like a dog with a bone. She wasn't going to release her hold on this case. I saw the way she snapped when I told her she was a bad PI. That had affected her even more than when I called her a whore. Whatever her other faults, she did care about her job.

I cringed at the memory. I didn't say things like that, especially not to a woman. I had not been myself in that apartment. As a defense mechanism, I had morphed into a monster of a man. I had just been so blind-sided by that stupid fucking notebook. I had been shocked and hurt, and so I had lashed out with whatever weapons came to hand.

I should have known better. I should have been more careful. I had somehow convinced myself that I knew her, just because we had insane chemistry. I didn't know her. I had met her only weeks ago, and pretty much everything had been a lie.

I was jolted back into the present when my bike drifted too close to the line and the car in the other lane honked at me. I cursed and looked for the nearest exit. It wasn't good to ride when my head was in such turmoil. My life was pretty shitty at the moment, but I still didn't want to be scraped off the pavement.

Once I was off the highway, I pulled into the parking lot

of a diner and parked my bike. I got off, but didn't go inside. I just leaned against the bike and thought. I forced myself to consider my relationship (if I could even still call it that) with Claire in chronological order. It was torture, but I ran through each and every detail.

It started that night at Blue Dog Saloon. Claire had been at the bar, and Moves had gone to her. She hadn't approached us first, but she probably would have at some point, just to get closer to Kim and Trey. She had been cute and personable. A little bit flirty, although back then Kim had been her priority. I should have remembered that. She hadn't been interested in me at all in the beginning. I was just a stepping stone on her way to cornering Trey. She hadn't even faked attraction back then.

I had known that at some point. I had been curious about her, but I had known nothing was likely to happen. Everything changed the night we caught Trey. I let out a bitter laugh as I recalled the fake date. As if that had been the only fake thing about Claire. I had thought that because I was helping her with the PI stuff, I was in on the joke. I had been allowed behind the curtain.

Instead, I was just like Trey. I was being deceived in Claire's con.

I wondered if she was already looking into Outlaw Souls at that point. I wished that I had read that notebook closer. In the moment, I was too overcome to glean more than the general details. I barely remembered the names. The missing girl was Zoe and the boy was Hector, but I couldn't recall their last names or their parents' names.

According to Claire's notes, they had gotten tangled up with bikers and then ran away. No word from them, but a lot of rumors flying around about drugs. Because that's what bikers did, according to people. We dealt drugs and we ruined young kids' lives.

I tried to remember how many pages of notes she had. There was a lot, but that was typical Claire. She was thorough. I snorted. I had to stop thinking about things like "typical Claire." I didn't know what was typical. I didn't know anything about the real Claire.

Maybe she already had the case the night we slept together. At the time, I hadn't thought Claire was being too aggressive. She was into me, just like I was into her, but she wasn't pursuing me with relentless determination. She had just seen where the night had taken her.

How long had it taken her to master that degree of nuance and subtlety? How many men had she seduced? How often had she practiced her delicate dance? I had been right that first time to sneak out before morning. If only I had left and never looked back. I should have stuck to my initial instinct and let Claire Brennan fall from my mind.

Instead, I had reconsidered. I had thought it would be harmless to hang out with her again. And how serendipitous it had been when she texted me? It was my lucky day. I hadn't even paused for a second to wonder why she was reaching out after two days of radio silence.

By that point, I was sure she was on the case against Outlaw Souls. I had been blind in the moment, but looking back it was so obvious. She had agreed to just hang out at her own home. It was quiet there. If we had gone out dancing again at a club, she would have had very little time to question me. If we had gone on a real date, that would have been too much hassle.

So Claire opted for the most efficient method of gleaning information. She didn't even have to leave her own home. I went to her, and I talked and talked about everyone's role and how our club operated.

I knew she couldn't do anything with what I had given her because Outlaw Souls was as clean as they came, but the fact that the whole time, she had her ears pricked for any shady details was repulsive to me. I cringed as I remembered how I had blabbered on and on about how we got gigs, how new pledges were brought into the fold, and how Moves kept everyone in line.

I frowned at that. Of all the things I had said to Claire, that was the only thing that edged on the controversial. As enforcer, Moves had to operate in some gray areas. He never crossed the line as far as I was concerned, but I wasn't sure Claire would see it like that.

If Claire was going to fixate on anyone in Outlaw Souls as the potential villain, it would be Moves. Which was total bullshit because he was at heart one of the best men I knew. It made me sick to my stomach that Claire would even suspect him of going after a sixteen-year-old girl.

The drug stuff was unfathomable as well. Moves only used violence to curtail drug dealing on our turf. He never left anyone with serious injuries. But then again, who knew if Claire saw it that way? She probably figured that Moves was beating up half of La Playa and dealing drugs to the other half while I fixed the books to make the money disappear.

I kicked the ground in frustration. I had to tell Moves and the others about this. We were going to have to look into what bikers were behind this, but I doubted we were going to have to look very far. This situation had Las Balas written all over it. Only people who didn't understand biker culture and the differences between our clubs would mix us up.

My brothers needed to know what Las Balas was doing.

Somehow we were going to have to curtail the drug dealing and possibly rescue a few teenagers. If those teenagers were even still within reach. It wasn't going to be a fun conversation. My brothers would never cut me off, but they wouldn't take it as no big deal that I had unwittingly brought a spy into our midst.

But first I had to continue replaying my past mistakes.

That night watching TV and talking had been the night things started to change for me. My feelings had started to grow. And the whole time she had just been waiting for me to fall asleep so she could jot down all her notes. Or had she? We hadn't talked about Outlaw Souls the whole night. We talked about TV, food, our lives. A range of topics.

That just showed how good Claire was at a con. She never forced Outlaw Souls into conversation. She let me think that everything was natural. That it was natural for us to just fall asleep in each other's arms. That it was natural for us to wake up and share breakfast and then just go for a ride.

First dates weren't supposed to be like that. They weren't supposed to last over twelve hours, and I wasn't supposed to fall that hard for a girl on the first date. But Claire had manipulated the whole thing so I didn't have a chance to stop and think. I should have tried to slow down, but instead I had surged ahead, positive that I had found someone special.

Then came the barbecue. That was the part that hurt the most. Thinking about how she had charmed all my brothers while the whole time searching for clues that weren't there.

I paused at that. I was right. There hadn't been any clues. Not even a hint of anything off about Outlaw Souls. If I knew one thing, it was that Claire wasn't stupid. She had to have seen that Outlaw Souls wasn't the type of club to dabble in criminal activity.

I thought back to this morning, as unpleasant as it was. I replayed the conversation. She had said something about Outlaw Souls. She had said they *were* the main suspects. She had said she knew they didn't do anything.

But she could have been lying. She might have wanted to cover her ass and say whatever she had to in order to salvage a connection to me so she could continue her sleuthing. Then later, she had said she would keep investigating, but she hadn't said she would keep investigating Outlaw Souls.

I growled in frustration. I couldn't trust anything she said, but even now, I wanted to think that she no longer suspected us. I tried to remember the notes. She wouldn't have lied in those notes. They had been detailed and precise and without bias, at least I could say that for Claire. She had written down a lot of no's in regard to Outlaw Souls: no drug paraphernalia, no mention of drugs, no signs of addiction.

So maybe she had cleared Outlaw Souls, but that didn't change the fact that she had been using me. I couldn't think in detail about the night before. Each memory of how I had held her and slowly undressed her was like a knife to the gut. She had responded to my touch, had given back to me, but it had all been in the relentless pursuit of her investigation. Even if she no longer suspected the Outlaw Souls, she had only agreed to be with me because of her job. That tainted her actions.

Another line she had said this morning came back to me in startling clarity: "I wasn't faking my feelings." She had said that. She had also said that last night was real for her, but I had responded with anger and hatred.

"Lies," I muttered. "She was lying."

But I was no longer as certain. The self-righteous fury of the morning was beginning to trickle away. I was just sad now. I felt empty. I had lost something, and I was beginning to fear that I had even had anything to begin with. A small stupid part of myself hoped that maybe she had meant it. Maybe she hadn't been faking.

I turned and got back on my bike. I couldn't think like that. Outlaw Souls was the priority right now. I had to push my sadness to the side and go to my brothers. There was no going back and correcting my mistakes. I had to keep moving forward. And if that meant freezing my heart forever, then so be it.

I reminded myself that I had recovered from betrayal before, I could do it again.

Only I had a sneaking suspicion that I was the one telling lies now.

TWENTY-FOUR
CLAIRE

I wished more than anything that I was the type of girl who could heal by eating her weight in chocolate and sobbing over a romantic comedy. Or a documentary about serial killers. I wasn't picky about what I watched while consuming chocolate, as long as it worked to distract me.

But that wasn't me.

Wallowing had never been my style. I had to take action. I could only heal if I stayed in motion. Maybe it wasn't healing. Maybe it was just forgetting. I didn't care. I just needed to move.

So I finally got up off the floor. I yanked on jeans and a T-shirt. I picked up my notebook from where Pin had slammed it on the table, and I held it in my hands. There were still two missing teenagers. There was still a drug ring. I still had to solve this investigation. It was all I had left.

Was it a fair trade? Was losing Pin worth this case?

"No," I whispered.

I shook my head and sat down on my couch. I couldn't think like that. I couldn't think about Pin or myself at all. The only way I could look at this investigation was if I cut myself completely out of it. I had to eradicate all my personal feelings and all my pain from the case.

Every moment I spent with Pin that wasn't somehow connected to this investigation, I had to push aside. Which meant most of the time with Pin had to be forgotten. When it came down to it, we really hadn't spent that much time thinking about Outlaw Souls. We had spent most of our time together sharing stories about ourselves, not to mention having passionate sex.

That had to be forgotten too. Pin could call me a whore all he wanted, but I knew that I had not been thinking about my job or the investigation at all when we had been intimate.

I gritted my teeth and shut my eyes. No more thoughts about me. I had to erase myself. I wondered if maybe I should have taken up meditation years ago to prepare for this moment. It was too late now. All I had was willpower, and that was going to have to be enough.

I opened my eyes and flipped open the notebook.

"The facts," I muttered to myself. "Just the facts."

Zoe had been dating a biker. Hector had been into bikes. They both ran away three months ago.

Outlaw Souls was a biker club, but they didn't deal drugs. At least most of them didn't, I was sure of that. I could not rule out the possibility that they had a few rogue members. As a whole though, they weren't that kind of club. Pin had told me that once, early on. But that statement implied that some biker clubs *were* that kind of club.

I gasped as I thought back to this morning. He had said something – what was it? I didn't want to think about this morning. I didn't want to be reduced to a sobbing mess again. But he had said something, right after he discovered the notebook.

It came back to me in a flash: "We didn't take anyone, we would never. We're not —"

And then he had said a name. He had been speaking so fast, and I had been so upset because he wasn't listening to me. And then right after he had accused me of being bad at my job, but I couldn't think of that.

It had been a name, I was certain. But it hadn't sounded familiar to my ears.

Las Balas.

It had been Spanish, I realized. I had lived in Southern California long enough to recognize that at least, but I had no idea what it meant. I leapt off the couch and ran to grab my computer from my desk. I opened it and typed the words into my search engine to find a translation.

The bullets.

That did sound familiar. Where had I heard that before? Had Pin mentioned it? I didn't think he had ever said something about bullets or guns. I would have noticed if he had because I was listening for that kind of language.

But I had heard it. I ran through my memories, trying to fast forward the more painful ones, until I paused at the barbecue. I had been in the bathroom, frustrated because nothing was making sense. I ran into Pin (fast forward through that), and then we had walked back out and seen Moves.

Who was leaving. Because there were some bullets that needed to be taken care of. Or something along those lines.

Had he said anything else? He had been tense, I remember, the lines of his face hardened. Pin had lowered his voice as well, but hadn't felt the need to discuss it at length. Instead, Pin had sat down with me and told me... other things that I didn't want to think about.

Bullets. Las Balas. The Outlaw Souls were *not* like Las Balas.

Another biker club. I could have slapped myself. Of course, I had considered that possibility, but all the parents kept chirping up with Outlaw Souls. But that could have been because that was the only biker club they had even heard of.

I turned back to my computer and threw myself into more research. It wasn't easy to find anything. It wasn't like biker clubs had websites or got mentioned in the news all the time, but the internet was a vast place and the mentions were there.

Las Balas was another club in La Playa. And they were trouble. All the things that had been missing when I was scouring the internet for details on Outlaw Souls were present. Las Balas were mentioned in a few police reports for assault and battery. Some neighborhood watch blogs mentioned them hanging around, possibly dealing drugs.

As far as I could tell, they were a smaller and newer club. Outlaw Souls were more established in the area, which was why Zoe and Hector's parents had fixated on their name. They had heard them mentioned more and made assumptions. That was my best guess anyway.

I stood up and began pacing around the room. Las Balas. I had to find them. I had to finish this case as soon as I could. I wasn't naive enough to think that if I took down Las Balas then Pin would take me back. What I had done was unforgivable. He had made that perfectly clear.

I wasn't going to get Pin back, but I could solve this case. I could at least redeem the Outlaw Souls' reputation. And get Zoe and Hector back home.

I was buzzing with adrenaline. I had to keep moving. My mind whirred through ways to get in touch with Las

Balas. At last, I decided to not overcomplicate it. One of the comments on a Reddit thread mentioned that Las Balas liked to hang out at a bar called Fisherman's Wharf (which was strange because it was nowhere near the beach). I mapped out a route and started to plan.

I didn't have to do anything stupid, but I needed to do something. If I just popped over to that bar, grabbed a drink and made some observations, I would be much farther along than I had been this morning.

It was a public place, after all. I was a smart girl, I could handle this. Besides, there was nothing to be gained by waiting. Tomorrow, the situation would be exactly the same.

I raced around my apartment, grabbing supplies and clothes while I dialed Veronica's number.

"Hey," she said. "What's up?"

"I'm doing some recon tonight," I said. "A place called the Fisherman's Wharf, just to see if I can get eyes on bikers for the missing teens case."

"The ones you were with last night?" Veronica asked.

We always kept each other appraised of the general details in our cases. It was good to have someone in the know. "No, it's a different club. Las Balas."

I heard clacking on the other end. Veronica was on her computer.

"Ok, I see it on the map," Veronica said. "Sketchy area."

"I know, I'm a big girl," I said.

"Don't need to remind me," Veronica said. "Just be careful and stay in contact. If you don't text for a while, you know I'll call out the hounds."

"Of course," I said.

After we hung up, I prepared for my role for the night. I pulled on an itty-bitty black leather mini-skirt and a low-cut camisole blouse. Then I decided on a long black blazer. It was a little formal, but it had deep pockets so my mace could be easily accessed. Besides, I wasn't going for the total bimbo look. I couldn't really pull that off, so I wanted to just look like an inebriated secretary who was looking for some thrills to spice up her drab life.

It's hard to fake drug addiction, so I wasn't even going to try. And I definitely wasn't going to stroll into the bar and ask for some heroin because that was about the same as screaming that you were an undercover cop.

I spent more time than usual on my makeup. I didn't usually wear a lot, but makeup could serve as good armor. A good amount of shimmery eyeshadow and dark eyeliner can go a long way towards masking expressions. Not to mention that red lipstick is a killer distraction. I didn't do anything attention-grabbing, just enough to hide behind.

I finished the look with some high-heeled boots. Not great for running, but I had no intention of needing to run tonight. I threw my notebook, an extra bottle of pepper spray, and a taser into my purse. I grabbed my phone and fiddled with it. I had the strangest urge to text Pin.

I would never expect a response, but I wanted to tell him what I was doing. I wanted him to know that I was at least trying to make things right. That now knew it was Las Balas. I had at least been a good enough PI to figure that out.

I also wanted him to know where I was. It was stupid, but I felt like I would be safer if Pin was aware of my movements. Like he cared.

But he didn't. Yesterday, he would have wanted to know. Hell, yesterday, he might have gone with me. Today, I could walk straight into hell, and he would probably cheer.

I shoved my phone into my bag. Veronica knew where I was going, and she would have my back. I didn't need Pin.

An hour later, I pulled into the lot of Fisherman's Wharf. I had stopped on the way to eat a quick meal from McDonald's in my car. I wasn't going to go into this on an empty stomach.

My heart started racing when I saw a row of bikes parked in the lot. This was it. I knew in my gut that I was going to find something in there. It might not be Zoe or Hector, but there was going to be some sign that I was on the right track.

I touched up my lipstick in my mirror before pulling my smaller handbag (wallet, phone, and taser inside) over my head. I touched my pocket again for my mace. I wasn't going to use it. I was going to walk in, order a drink, look around, maybe flirt with a guy, then hightail it out of there.

I knew Fisherman's Wharf was a whole other level of sketch as soon as I walked through the door. The bartender was a dead giveaway. At Blue Dog Saloon, the barkeep had been grimy, perhaps a bit grouchy, but he had been upfront and focused on his business. The bartender at Fisherman's Wharf took one look at me and gave me a lecherous smirk.

If I hadn't already seen a group of leather-clad men huddled in the corner booth, I would have turned around and walked right out. But I was too close to give up. I walked up to the bar and hopped on a stool. I didn't keep my head down or try to be subtle. The bar was slow, so there was no use trying to hide.

"Haven't seen you before, sweetheart," the bartender said.

His voice was slick and oily, and he stared at my cleavage without shame. I gave him a small shrug and pouted my lips. As if I had a really rough day, and maybe I was slightly ashamed that I had a taste for bad guys.

"Just thought I'd try someplace new," I said. "Is that a problem?"

He snorted. "No problem at all. What can I get you?"

"Gin and tonic, please," I said. I was going to take one sip, that was all. Then I would pretend to get a text from an ex.

While the creep of a bartender went to make my drink, I glanced around the room. A few of the bikers had clocked me, but they didn't seem that interested.

No one resembles Zoe. No Hector, either.

But there was one young woman. I recognized her at once. Grace Vasquez. The older girl who had played volleyball with Zoe before getting involved with a biker and running away a year before. She was eighteen by now, so not really my problem, but Zoe's parents had suspected she had introduced her daughter to the bikers.

It was definitely her. She had bleached the ends of her dark hair, and her skin looked a lot more sallow than it had in her yearbook photo, but it was Grace alright. And she had been using. I would bet the contents of my wallet on it. I didn't think she was high just that moment, but her addiction was evident in the dark circles beneath her eyes that no amount of concealer could hide and the puffiness of her cheeks. I knew if she were to roll up her sleeves, I would probably see puncture marks on her arms.

I looked back down at the table. I had what I had come for. Grace was here, which meant that Zoe was tied up with Las Balas. Hector too most likely. I would need backup to start trailing them, but now I knew where I could start.

The bartender placed the gin and tonic down, and I paid as fast as I could. I was pulling out my phone, all ready to do a small fake reaction to a booty call, when my neck prickled. There was someone behind me.

I told myself to remain calm and turned. It was a tall guy with messy brown hair. He gave me a smile that made my blood curdle. He wasn't bad-looking, quite attractive even. But I could tell whatever he wanted with me wasn't anything good.

"Hey Claire," he said.

I froze. I flicked my eyes around the room and saw that now all the bikers were regarding me from their side of the room. The three other customers had their heads down while the bartender was still smirking on the other side of the bar.

He knew my name. It was time to run.

I scooted off the chair and turned for the door, but the man grabbed my arm. In a matter of seconds, he had ripped my purse over my head. I started breathing heavy. This was bad, really bad. No one in this bar was going to help me, and he had just acquired my phone, my wallet, and my taser. All I had was my pepper spray in my pocket, but if I whipped that out now, one of the other bikers was going to yank it off me before I could get to the door.

This wasn't supposed to happen. How the hell did they know who I was?

"Oh no, you're not leaving so soon," the man said. "We've been wondering when you would show up here."

I looked up and froze. He had a scar on his cheek. Liz had said Zoe's older boyfriend had a scar. Fuck, this was bad. This was really bad.

He reached up and placed a finger in the middle of my forehead, where my brow was creased. I flinched away, but he only smiled.

"Oh Claire, we've heard all about you," he said. "Sniffing around asking questions about Zoe and Hector."

"How do you know my name?" I snapped.

My voice came out somewhat steady, much to my relief. I was desperate to know how they knew me. It was also dawning on me that the only way I was getting out of this was by keeping them calm and waiting for an opportunity.

"You really thought you could run around asking Hector's old friends about him *and* start fucking an Outlaw Soul, and we wouldn't notice?" he asked. "How dumb do you think we are?"

My heart sank. He knew a lot. Hector must have still been in contact with one of his stupid friends who was probably about to run away to deal drugs as well.

"By the way," the man said, his hand still gripping my arm as he pulled me across the room. "I was impressed by how quickly you hopped in bed with Pin, he's notoriously hard to get."

The whole time his voice remained low and steady, almost as if he was commenting on nothing more serious than the weather, but I wasn't fooled. This man was a predator. He opened a back door and dragged me through, his buddies following behind. We entered a small and dingy room. I was in so much trouble.

The man let me go and pointed at a chair. I sat down. Not like I had a chance of fighting them off. Besides, they needed to think I was terrified. I let my fear show on my face. If they thought I had given up, they would be more lax.

"I am sorry you had to suck Pin's dick, and it was all for nothing," he said.

I wanted to slap him. Hard. Instead, I bit down on my tongue and remained silent. I couldn't let him rile me. Veronica knew where I was. If I didn't text her in thirty minutes, she was going to launch into action. I just had to survive until then.

My stomach clenched. Did I really think this had come

to life and death? I looked up at the sneer on the leader's face, and I knew that this man was capable of anything.

"Where's Zoe?" I asked.

From the corner, Grace Vasquez scoffed and rolled her eyes. "Don't tell her anything, Wreck."

His name was Wreck. Even in my dire straits, I noted how appropriate the nickname was. Wreck turned to me and ran his cold eyes up and down my body. I wanted to throw up.

"I commend your commitment," he said. "But you should really know when to give up."

"I'll drop the case," I said. "Zoe and Hector will be legal adults soon anyway. It will fade away. I swear, I'll never come near your club again."

I shrugged and tried to look like I could care less. When in fact, if I managed to walk away from this, I was going to do everything in my power to burn Las Balas to the ground. But it was a very big "if."

Wreck let out a soft little laugh at my bid for freedom.

"Sweetheart, I don't believe a word out of your pretty little mouth," he said. "And trust me, you're much more useful to us right where you are."

I furrowed my brow. Wreck leaned in close and picked up a strand of my hair and ran it through his fingers. His scent was sweet like rose flowers, making me gag.

"After all, what do you think Pin would hand over if he knew we had you?" Wreck asked.

My eyes widened. Pin had access to the Outlaw Souls' funds. He knew everything about the club and their territory. If Las Balas managed to blackmail Pin, that was pretty much the nail in Outlaw Souls coffin.

My self-control snapped, and I spat directly into Wreck's eye. I would have head-butted him if I hadn't been sure it would just end with my concussion. But seeing the glob of spit land in his face was satisfying enough.

He cursed and reeled back.

"You bitch," he hissed.

I saw stars when he backhanded me across the face. The pain stung, but I breathed through it. Spitting on him had been a mistake. I was going to have to control myself better if I wanted to get out of this.

"Watch her," Wreck snapped.

His cronies stepped up and leered down at me, while Wreck regained his composure.

"I'll be back, Claire," Wreck said. "And I hope you'll treat me with a bit more respect."

He bared his teeth in a smile one last time before turning and heading out of the room. I kept my head down in a gesture of defeat.

But I wasn't defeated.

No one was going to come rescue me. I had to get out of this on my own.

TWENTY-FIVE
PIN

"Fuck," Moves said.

I watched as my friend paced back and forth in the back room of the Blue Dog Saloon.

"Fuck," he said. "Fuck, fuck, fuck."

For the past five minutes, he had said little else.

I had told him everything. I texted him and drove straight to the Blue Dog Saloon. The whole story had poured out of me: Claire's investigation into missing teenagers, her notes on the Outlaw Souls, our fight, and how I was pretty sure Las Balas were the real culprits.

I had tried to keep my emotions out of it, but it was hard to hide my pain, especially when Moves was staring at me with a look of utter shock.

"Fuck," Moves said.

"Enough," I said. "We need to decide what to do."

"Ok, give me a sec," he said, throwing his arms out. "I just can't believe Claire was playing you. I mean, I thought she was for real."

"Well, she wasn't," I snapped.

I couldn't believe Moves wanted to focus on my joke of

a relationship in all this. We needed to be thinking about Las Balas. We had to consider how best to defend our own reputation.

"Are you sure?" Moves asked. "I mean, she would have to be one hell of an actress."

"Moves, I don't wanna talk about Claire." I could tell Moves didn't want to leave it alone, but he ran a hand through his hair and let out a sigh.

"I told you that dealer was young," Moves said. "Wish I could say I was surprised, but Las Balas are rotten through and through."

"We need to tell Ryder and the others," I said after nodding. "And then we need to figure out how to extract those kids with the least amount of collateral."

"It's gonna be hard," Moves said. "I don't want any confrontation, but it might come to that."

Moves leaned back against the table and squinted his eyes. "It would be best to move fast. You call Ryder yet?"

"I called but he's not picking up," I said.

"Shit, he might be out of town," Moves muttered. "He mentioned he might go for a ride last night."

I crossed my arms. That wasn't good. We had to move soon. I couldn't explain why, but it felt like every second that passed, things got worse and worse. Something wasn't right in our territory, and we had to fix it.

It could have been the situation, but it also could have been my desperation to not think about Claire. As long as I was focused on the drugs and the kids, I didn't have to consider Claire and everything that had been said that morning.

How was it only a few hours ago? It already felt like another day, another person. I wanted to throw up when I thought of what I had said to her. In anger, I had reached for the words I knew would hurt the most, but now I wanted to take back each and every one. I wanted to listen to her as well. I wasn't sure if I would believe her, but I still wanted to hear her side.

"I can reach out to my contacts," Moves said. "Try and ask around."

I looked up and forced myself to focus. What was done was done. It was over between me and Claire. Moves cursed again. He was pacing now too, buzzing with frantic energy. He was itching to take action as well, and I was grateful to have him by my side.

"But as soon as I start asking around, they'll hear," he said. "Las Balas get word of things *fast*."

"You know," Moves said, turning to me and going still. "A third party could help, if you reached out to Claire and her PI firm. All we would have to do is push them in the right direction and tell them what to expect."

"No," I said. "No way. I don't want her involved at all."

"She already is involved," Moves pointed out. "Besides, she's a PI, she has resources. Even police contacts."

"I told her to stop the investigation," I said.

"And you think she listened?" Moves asked.

He raised a cynical brow to indicate that he seriously doubted Claire was going to just call it a day on this investigation.

"Better that we give her a tip," Moves said. "Or else she's fumbling in the dark."

"She thought it was us," I said. "Do you not get it? She was using me to spy on Outlaw Souls!"

Moves twisted his mouth, and I could tell he was going to say something I didn't like.

"But it wasn't us," Moves said. "She was just following a lead, and now we can help give her another lead. Her PI firm will help us out by taking care of Las Balas, and we all win."

It wasn't the first time I wanted to hit Moves. His obstinate habit of saying whatever was on his mind and oversimplifying every situation drove me crazy.

"There is no winning," I growled. "Not for me."

"Call me a hopeless romantic," Moves said, raising his hands in the air. "But I really believed in you two."

"Are you fucking kidding me?" I snapped. "It was all a lie, everything she did was so she could sniff for dirt on me and my brothers."

"Are you sure?" Moves said.

I gaped at him. I could not believe he was siding with Claire.

"Would you be so casual about it if you were in my shoes?" I asked. "If you found out the woman you were with had a whole other agenda."

"Of course not," Moves said. "And I'm with you, it's just a lot to take in."

I sighed. "A lot to take in" was the understatement of the year.

"I'm not saying you should take her back or forgive her or whatever," Moves said. "I'm just saying that giving her the relevant information would be a good way to end this whole shitshow quickly. Then you can move on."

The idea of moving on seemed so ludicrous to me that I almost laughed aloud. Moves had a point though. If we moved against Las Balas, it wouldn't be pretty. But if we pushed Claire and her contacts to move against them, those teens actually stood a chance.

"I know she hurt you," Moves said. "And I hate that you had to go through this, but maybe you need to deal with this first, and then we can get drunk, ok?"

I managed a small laugh at that. Moves always had a plan, even if it was flimsy. "I'll call her."

The phone rang out. It wasn't surprising, but something didn't sit right. Of course, I had left her furious and crying, so it made sense that she wouldn't pick up. I told myself that as I typed out a text:

We need to talk about your investigation.
Moves and I are pretty sure we know where the missing kids are.

It was a pretty measly message, considering everything that had gone down. Yet I didn't know what else to say. I longed to apologize for what I had said earlier, but my pride wouldn't let me. And no matter what, I couldn't apologize over text. Moves was right, I had to deal with the most pressing issue first.

Five minutes later, Claire had not responded to the message.

"Something's off," I muttered.

"What do you mean?" Moves said. "Give her some time."

He was lounging in a chair and playing on his own phone. I couldn't stop walking back and forth. "You don't understand. Claire – she's obsessed with this case, she would have responded by now, if just for the information."

Moves looked up. "She could be in the shower."

I couldn't even respond to his weak attempt to come up with an excuse.

"Maybe I should go to her place," I muttered.

Moves was about to answer when we heard footsteps pounding across the barroom. A moment later, the door swung open to reveal Kim, her helmet under her arm. She was breathing heavy.

"Thank God you're here," she said. "I need back-up, Claire's in trouble."

My heart stopped. Moves was on his feet and grabbing his helmet and jacket in an instant.

"What happened?" My voice was cold and foreign. It didn't sound like it belonged to me.

"Not sure, but she's been on a case, and she went into Las Balas territory tonight," Kim said. "She told her partner she was headed to Fisherman's Wharf and left my number just in case, but her partner called me to say Claire hasn't responded to her texts in almost twenty minutes."

All in a rush, my heart started pounding again. If Claire had walked into Fisherman's Wharf, that meant she was a few steps ahead of us. Somehow she had figured out that Las Balas were behind this.

It also meant she was in trouble.

"I told her to stay out of it," I hissed, even as I grabbed my helmet from Moves and headed for the door.

"Look, I don't know what went down between you two," Kim said. "But the way I see it, you just let your woman wander into the lion's den unprotected."

We all headed to the door. Kim could lecture me all she wanted, but we knew we were going to move as a unit. We had no choice.

"Hey, Kim, back off," Moves said. "He's hurting."

"Whatever," Kim snapped. "All I know is Claire had my back, now I need to have hers."

We jumped onto our bikes and were roaring across town. We had to get to Fisherman's Wharf before something bad happened. Although if Claire hadn't texted Veronica back, something bad might have already happened. Claire had explained how she and Veronica had a system during cases. They always told each other where they were and agreed to stay in constant contact.

I revved my engine and urged my bike to go faster. I didn't know why Claire had gone to Fisherman's Wharf. She must have been telling the truth when she said that she no longer suspected Outlaw Souls. Then she must have done some more digging and put two and two together. Somehow she had figured out their headquarters. And, of course, she had waltzed right in. Because she was Claire, and she would do whatever it took to solve a case.

And I had only pushed her in that direction when I accused her of being bad at her job. When I had refused to listen to her. I should have at least listened. She had hurt me, and I knew what she had done was wrong, but I hadn't been faking anything. My feelings for her were real, and I couldn't stop caring about her. So I should have made sure she was ok.

But now I could pay the ultimate price.

Las Balas were unpredictable. They were led by Wreck, a biker with a dark past and a cruel sense of humor. If they somehow figured out who Claire was, they would be ruthless.

They must have figured it out. That was the only explanation for why she had not responded to Veronica's messages.

I ground my teeth underneath my helmet as we sped closer and closer to Fisherman's Wharf. I didn't have the time to dwell over what had happened this morning. I could only think about one thing, and it was making sure Claire was safe.

And if she wasn't, I was going to tear Las Balas limb from limb until she was.

TWENTY-SIX
CLAIRE

"I wanna make a deal," I said.

Wreck had returned to the back room after about twenty minutes. I didn't know what he had been doing, but I prayed he hadn't reached out to Pin yet.

Pin was good. Too good for me, that was for sure. No matter how much Pin hated me, he wouldn't stand by if he knew Las Balas had me. He would do the honorable thing, no matter the cost. I couldn't live with that. So I had to negotiate myself out of this before Pin was sucked into the mess.

Wreck raised his brow and looked down at where I sat, arms and legs crossed. "Honey, you don't exactly have a winning hand right now."

I bit back a retort. If he called me "honey" or "sweetheart" one more time, I was going to whip out my mace. "I have information on Outlaw Souls. And you're more likely to get it from me than from Pin."

Wreck paused. He grabbed a chair and dragged it across the floor until it was right across from me. He had three other bikers in the room, all men. Grace Vasquez had vanished.

Wreck sat down and leaned forward, his knees almost touching mine. I kept eye contact with him. I didn't need him to bite on this deal. I just needed him to listen long enough for Veronica to call in the cavalry. It had been long enough, she would be concerned. I just hoped she didn't show up alone. This situation required back-up.

"Pin pretty much hates me," I said with a shrug. "He figured out I was using him, although he doesn't know the details of the case."

"That's a funny turn of events," Wreck said. "Because I heard from my sources that he was positively smitten with you."

I frowned. How much did Wreck know? What had he seen? And who were his sources? If I got out of this, I would have to let Outlaw Souls know they had a mole.

Instead of letting my questions show on my face, I gave Wreck a wry smile. "After barely a week? I'm good, but I'm not that good."

Wreck tipped back his head and laughed. The sound made my stomach curdle, but I had to play along. I had to make him believe that I didn't care about Pin or the Outlaw Souls at all. I was just out for myself.

"So tell me, sweetheart," Wreck said. "What exactly did you have in mind?"

I shrugged and studied my fingernails. I needed to take my time with this discussion, but not dilly-dally so much as to make Wreck suspicious. He had my phone after all. Texts from Veronica wouldn't show on my lock screen, but if he decided to make me log in so he could double-check, I was in trouble. He could make me text a fake message saying I was fine.

"I give you what I got on Outlaw Souls," I said. "You let me go, and I'll go find more for you. Pin wasn't the only biker I got along with."

Wreck snorted. I cringed on the inside at the way he assessed me. Let him think I was a slut who would sleep with anything to get what I wanted. He needed to think that.

"And how will I know you won't go running to your PI friends or even back to Pin?" he asked.

"You don't," I said. "But I can give you enough dirt on Outlaw Souls here and now that the risk is worth it. Trust me."

My mind was scrambling to come up with something juicy. I wish I knew more about the rivalry between the two clubs so I could at least think up an enticing lie.

Moves, I thought. Moves had to be one of their biggest enemies. I could tell them where he lived. A fake address since I didn't have the real one. It was pretty messed up, but worth a try. Or I could tell them something about the accounting. I had never even glimpsed at Pin's books, but I could make something up, surely.

"It's an interesting proposition," Wreck said. "But I think I have a better idea."

I frowned. I got the sense that I didn't want to know what "better" meant to Wreck.

"I'm just thinking how much I might enjoy spending time with you, Claire," Wreck said. "You really are a delight."

He touched my bare knee with the back of his finger, and it took everything in me not to shudder. So that's how he wanted to play this? He wanted to think I would at least consider the possibility of hopping in bed with him. It made sense that Wreck needed his ego to be stroked.

"And I'm sure it would drive Pin absolutely crazy," he said. "To see you hanging all over me."

He was wrong there. Pin would probably think I had found my match. He would think me and Wreck were bottom-feeders who were meant for each other.

"It might." I glanced up at Wreck from beneath my lashes and gave him a coy smile.

God, I hated this. But if it was my way out, so be it. I just hoped all I had to do was flirt. If Wreck tried to take it any further... I blocked that thought process.

Just survive the next hour. Just survive.

"Alright, sweetheart, tell me," Wreck said. "What deep dark secret do you have on the Outlaw Souls."

"You know Moves, right?" I asked. "He wants in on the dealing."

The words just spilled out. That was good though, it made them sound natural. And I could tell from Wreck's reaction that I had his attention.

"He's straight," one of his buddies grunted from the corner. "As straight as they come."

"I don't know him that well, it's true," I said with a little shrug. "But I imagine all that time he's spent chasing your dealers out of Souls territory has made him hungry for a little piece of the pie."

I hoped Moves would forgive me for maligning him with this hogwash. I could tell I had hit a note with Las Balas. It was because that was how they would think. They were greedy assholes who wanted whatever they could get, and it didn't matter how they got it.

"I overheard him on the phone at an Outlaw Souls barbecue," I said. "He was around the corner, but I heard him telling someone it was almost time to move product. Move it into Las Balas turf."

They were scared of Moves, I could tell. Pin had told me what a threat Moves could be, and he was the last person Las Balas wanted as competition.

"The way I see it, you need to either eradicate him," I said. "Or get him to join you. He could be your greatest asset or your biggest threat."

Until that moment, I truly did not know I had the ability to spiel off such nonsense under duress. If I hadn't been so terrified, I would have been impressed with myself.

Wreck wasn't convinced, but he was considering it. He gave me a hard look. This time he wasn't assessing my body in a lecherous way or teasing me. He was trying to gauge my motives. I pressed my lips together and held eye contact. "It's awfully convenient that you just happened to overhear this information about Moves."

Wreck was smarter than he looked. That was what made him so dangerous.

"Feel free to ignore it," I said. "Don't blame me when Moves takes over your whole track."

With a snarl, Wreck surged forward until his face was inches from mine. He gripped my chin in his hand, and terror coursed through me. "I don't like your bitchy tone, sweetheart."

Then there was shouting from outside. Footsteps pounded on the other side of the door. The bikers in the room were instantly on high alert. I saw one slide a knife from his belt.

Unexpected visitors. Wreck gripped me even tighter, but I had to make a move, it was now or never.

I still had an arm free, and I yanked my mace out of my pocket while kicking Wreck hard in the shins. Then I took aim and sprayed, a direct hit to his eyes.

As Wreck reeled back, three things happened all at once.

First, the door burst open, revealing Pin, Moves, and Kim looking like angels of death, coming to rescue me.

Second, the other Las Balas bikers took action, two facing off against the invaders and one lurching towards me.

And third, Pin saw me.

He saw me caught between a blind but livid Wreck and a hulking Las Balas biker.

He saw me, and in that instant, I knew I was safe. I was going to make it out, and I was going to be alright. Then everything happened very fast.

I turned my mace at the other biker's face before he could even get a good grip on my arm. Wreck was lunging at me, but Pin bowled into him from behind.

They tumbled to the ground in a mess of limbs, but thanks to my solid aim with the mace, Pin ended up on top. I wrenched myself away from the biker and scrambled over to Kim. She grabbed my hand and yanked me towards the door.

Meanwhile, Moves was making short work of the other bikers. He was something to behold. In quick abrupt movements, he dropped the one biker with a well-placed punch to the face, then moved onto the next. Every movement was precise and efficient, as if he had done the same fight over and over, every day for years.

I realized Kim was trying to pull me out of the room, but I held put. I wasn't leaving Pin.

"Claire, we need to get out now," Kim said.

"Not without Pin," I said.

"Pin, enough!" Kim shrieked.

I turned to see that Pin had turned Wreck's face into a

bloody mess, but he showed no sign of slowing down. Some sort of primal rage had come over him. For me, I realized. He was protecting me.

"Pin!" I yelled.

Only then did he turn. He saw me, and the anger receded from his face. He pushed himself off Wreck and crossed the room to grip my head in his hands.

"Are you hurt?" he murmured. "Tell me if you're hurt."

"I'm fine," I said. "But please, let's leave."

Pin circled an arm around my waist, and I knew that I never wanted him to let go.

He guided me out of the bar and into the lot. He shoved a helmet on my head, and I got on his bike behind him. Then we were off, the whole violent scene at Fisherman's Wharf feeling like a fever dream.

I clutched Pin's chest with everything I had in me, the air chilling my bare legs. He had come for me. Even though I had done nothing to deserve it, he had barged into enemy territory. Because he was a good man, and he did the right thing.

I knew once we were in safety, his obligation would be done. He would go back to hating me. But I couldn't let him. I knew now that I had to fight for him. I had to try to make him understand that I hadn't been faking. I had to let him know that I loved him.

The bikers pulled over in another lot. Blue Dog Saloon. Back to where it all started. When I stepped off the bike, my legs were weak. As soon as I took my helmet off, I started apologizing.

"I'm so sorry," I said. "Pin, Moves, Kim, I didn't mean for that to happen – I was just doing recon, but they recognized me somehow."

Pin tossed my helmet aside and gripped my shoulders. I realized he wasn't even listening to my apology, he was surveying me for damage. He stiffened as he saw the growing bruise on the side of my face. "Did he hit you?"

I shivered at his voice, low and lethal.

"I'm fine," I whispered. "Truly, I'm fine."

"I should have killed him," Pin said.

"No," I said. "I don't want to be responsible for a body. I've done enough."

"Claire, don't apologize," Moves said. "We should have told you about Las Balas as soon as we could. We figured they were responsible. If we had told you, you wouldn't have had to go solo."

"And it's all good now," Kim said. "You can call in back-up to get those missing teens out if you can. I already filled in Veronica."

"Veronica called you?" I asked.

"Your partner's a smart woman," Moves said.

The whole time, Pin didn't take his eyes off of me.

"Why don't you guys head inside to talk," Kim said. "We'll stay out here and make some calls."

I threw Kim a grateful look. She must have sensed that I had a lot to say to Pin. He released my shoulders, but kept his hand on my back as he guided me into the back room of the Blue Dog Saloon. The whole time, he didn't say a word.

My heart couldn't slow down. I was already dreading the inevitable moment he was going to let go of me. One dramatic rescue couldn't erase what I had done. But he had to know. I had to tell him how I felt. "Pin, I –"

Before I could finish my sentence, he turned and enclosed me in a massive hug. I nearly sobbed with relief as I pressed my face into his chest and wrapped my arms around him. For several minutes, I just let him hold me.

Like a budding flower, hope began to bloom in my chest. This couldn't all mean nothing. Maybe there was something to salvage from the mess I had made.

I leaned back, looked up into his beautiful face, and took a deep breath.

TWENTY-SEVEN

PIN

The minute I saw Claire in Wreck's filthy hands, my entire world stopped.

It froze, suspended in time, as I saw my woman being manhandled by the worst piece of scum I knew. Then, when it started moving again, all I saw was red. A fury rose from somewhere deep inside me. It was a primal wrath that came from the need to protect what was mine.

If Claire hadn't called out my name, I wouldn't have stopped beating up Wreck. It had almost been too easy to take him down, thanks to Claire's pepper spray. It was pretty classic, I had to admit. Leave it to Claire to do half the work.

I knew that I was still mad at her. What she had done didn't just disappear. But the urgent situation had forced that aside for the time being. Some things were too important. Claire's safety was too important.

Even back in the Blue Dog Saloon, I couldn't let her go. I had to reassure myself that she was whole and solid in my arms. I had envisioned so many awful scenarios on that ride over, I had to feel the physical proof to make sure she was ok.

She leaned back and looked up at me, but I didn't take my hands off her shoulders. She kept her hands on my waist as well. I hated looking at her face, where a bruise was growing on the side. It looked like he had only struck her once, but that was one too many times. I would never forgive Wreck for this. I would make sure Las Balas never had a day of peace for the rest of their sorry existence.

"Pin, I have to tell you some things," Claire said. "I know you have no reason to listen, but is it ok if I tell you some things?"

I nodded. This time, I wanted to listen. I had been going in circles all day after our fight, and the only thing I was sure of was that I needed to hear her side of things.

"I got the assignment after we had slept together the first time," Claire said. "You can ask my boss or Veronica, ask anyone you need to, I want you to know the facts."

"I don't need witnesses," I said.

"No, you do," Claire said. "Or you deserve the truth, and I hate that I didn't tell you the truth from the beginning, so now I want to make sure you have it."

I nodded. I would check with her boss if she wanted me to, but I could see in Claire's eyes that this was the truth.

"I just want you to know that the first time we slept together, it was because I wanted to," Claire said. "I liked you, and yes, I thought of it as a casual hook-up, but it had nothing to do with my job or anything."

Claire took a trembling breath, and a single tear fell from her eye. I reached up and wiped it from her cheek. Claire's lips formed a soft smile at the tender touch.

"Then I got the assignment, and it was the kind of case I had been craving," Claire said. "It was big and complicated and important, so I texted you to hang out. The parents suspected Outlaw Souls, and I was desperate to get information. "I need you to know that I didn't intend to go very far with you. I'm not – I wouldn't –"

She stammered for the right words, and my heart went out to her. She wasn't defensive or angry like she had been this morning. She was laying herself bare.

"I would never sleep with someone I didn't want to," Claire said. "That's not me."

"I know," I said. "I should never have called you what I did this morning, and I'm sorry."

"Stop!" Her eyes were wide and she had put on an indignant face. "You have to let me finish my apology."

I had to smile, her expression was so funny. I nodded to indicate that she should go on.

"You were so easy to talk to that night, and the next morning was so fun," Claire said. "I felt so guilty, but I also was consumed by the case. Then you invited me to the barbecue, and I *knew* that night the Outlaw Souls were clean. I could tell by the way everyone operated and acted that it couldn't be you guys.

She breathed out, tears welling up. "And I know you might not believe me, but that's ok. I know I fucked up by not telling you about the investigation that night. If you walk away and never talk to me again, that's fine. I just have to tell you that what we did and said that night meant something to me. It was real and it was the first time I've ever felt anything like that."

Claire was crying in earnest now. Tears poured from her eyes, and her cheeks and nose turned red. I had never seen Claire lose control. She was always so quick and composed. Her cries made me want to bundle her up in my arms and hold her for days.

"I was going to tell you in the morning," Claire said. "I made up my mind that night that in the morning, I would come clean. I would explain everything and beg you to forgive me for lying, and then I hoped you might even help me. But it was so stupid of me to think what I had done was forgivable."

She took a great heaving breath. Then she pulled away to wipe her tears from her face. My arms instantly ached with the desire to hold her again.

Fear, sharp and intense, raced through me. She was going to walk away now. She had confessed, and now she recognized that too much had happened for her to stay. She was going to leave, and I was going to miss her, because I wanted her.

I couldn't deny it anymore. She had done what she did because she was Claire. She was passionate about her work, she was ambitious, and she led that misguide. But she always recognized her errors. She was the woman for me, and I couldn't condemn her for being herself.

"I love you," she said.

For the second time in an hour, my entire world stopped.

"I know it can't fix anything, but it's the truth," Claire said. "I fell in love with you, and that's why I went after Las Balas. I had to at least try and make things right. I know you might need some time, but I want you to know that I love you, and I want to fight for you."

She clasped her hands in front of her chest and took one last breath. When she looked up at me, there was only one answer I could give.

I grabbed her to me and kissed her as hard as I could. It was fierce and messy, and I could tell Claire was shocked by her sharp intake of breath, but I needed her to know how much I cared. I pulled her against my chest, and Claire tipped her head back as she wrapped her arms around my neck and clung to me like she would never let go.

At last, I pulled away and looked down at her. Her lips were parted in a little O of surprise.

"I love you," I said. "Everything you did – it's forgiven, as long as you can forgive me for what I said this morning. I shouldn't have stormed out, I should have listened."

"Pin," she gasped. "Are you – ?"

"I'm sure," I said. "You are the only one for me, I knew it as soon as I left you, but I couldn't admit until I saw you pepper spraying Wreck."

Claire burst out laughing. I couldn't help but smile along.

"You really shouldn't find it so funny," I said.

"I know," Claire gasped. "I was terrified."

Her laughter trailed up as she looked up at me. "But then you came. And I wasn't scared at all."

My heart swelled as I leaned down to kiss her once more.

"I love you," I said. "I'll never stop."

EPILOGUE: CLAIR

ONE YEAR LATER

I typed up my final note on my latest case and then leaned back in my chair.

This one had been a good one. A child had been missing for almost two years. Police had given up even though there was no body. I took it on a few weeks ago and today we found her. She had been kidnapped and wasn't in the best shape, but she was alive and back with her parents.

All my cases in the past year had been similar. After I tracked down Zoe and Hector and busted the Las Balas drug ring, the LA Times ran a huge piece that put me on the top of the list for any and all missing persons cases. It was what I had always wanted: the in-depth profile of top PI Claire Brennan.

It had been nice, I couldn't deny it. But I didn't care about the accolades. I just cared about making sure Zoe, who had gotten addicted to heroin, got the help she needed. And that Hector met some of the Outlaw Souls so he could learn how to love bikes and be a real man.

Pin had gone crazy over the article. He had even

printed it out and framed it to hang on my wall above my desk. He could be dorky like that. I loved it.

I checked my phone and saw that he had texted me:

You still be home by 7?

I checked my watch and texted back in the affirmative. We still had our own places, but we spent every night together. He came to mine to stock up my fridge and cook, or I went to his place where he had cleared out half his closet for me.

I never thought that I would last a year in a serious relationship. I thought I would feel trapped or bored or anxious. But with Pin, it wasn't even hard. Yes, we had our moments, but we were always honest with each other. We always found a way through the challenges.

When I got antsy, he just took me out to his bike, and we drove until I was smiling again.

He understood me, and I understood him. Both of us had mistrusted relationships before, and maybe we still did have that baggage. Maybe we did doubt the idea of relationships as a whole. But we did trust each other. I had never lied to Pin once after the first deception, and I knew he was honest with me. We told each other how we were feeling instead of keeping it bottled up inside.

We made each other happy. Just the sight of Pin, bent over his accounting books on my kitchen table made me grin from ear to ear. And every time he saw me, Pin couldn't keep his hands off me. We had found a way to make the relationship work. I knew that my life would never be boring as long as Pin was by my side.

When I got back to my apartment door, I fumbled with

the keys. Before I could even put them in the door, it swung open.

Pin stood smiling. I knew something was up right away. Behind him on the table, there were candles lit and two glasses of red wine.

He grabbed my hand and pulled me in. My heart started to pick up. We had talked about forever before. I had told him I wanted him for the rest of my life.

But we had never discussed details. The closest we had gotten to talking about a timeline or any sort of plan was a budgeting spreadsheet Pin had made. Which, I had to admit, had been weirdly romantic. It had been comforting seeing that he planned for us to get our own apartment at some point.

Before I could say anything, Pin had dropped down on one knee.

I never thought I would be the type of girl to erupt into butterflies at the sight of an engagement ring, but it turns out I never fully knew myself until I met Pin.

When he popped open the box to reveal the ruby ring, I gasped and clamped one hand over my mouth.

"Claire Brennan, I have loved you almost from the moment I first saw you," Pin said.

"Yes," I said. "Yes."

"I haven't even asked!" Pin cried.

"Well, my answer is yes." I started pulling on his hand, trying to yank him to his feet so I could kiss him.

"Claire, will you marry me?" Pin blurted as fast as he could.

"Yes!" I screamed, launching myself into his arms.

I vowed to never let go.

The End.

Dear reader,

I can't thank you enough for reading this book! I hope you enjoyed reading it as much I enjoyed writing it. It would mean the world to me if you took a minute to leave me an honest review in Amazon.

If it weren't for passionate readers like yourself that give me the opportunity to fulfill my dreams as a full time author doing what I feel like I was born to do...being creative, writing books and sharing it with beautiful people like you.

Thank you!
Hope Stone

Do you want to read more from the Outlaw Souls MC Series?

Book 3 centers around the Road Captain of the Outlaw Souls MC, Raul "Trainer' Lopez and a newly single mother named Erica.

I wasn't looking for a love connection.

But I didn't count on Trainer.

Black leather. Intricate tattoos. Sculpted body.

He looked like trouble that I didn't need.

Too bad he proved impossible to resist.

I found myself falling into bed with the tough biker.

But I had a dangerous secret...

Getting attached was a bad idea because I had trouble looking for me.

And I had to keep my son safe, no matter what.

EPILOGUE: CLAIR

I fled to La Playa to escape a nightmare.
Was it possible to find a future here with a good man?
Or would my past catch up to me and ruin everything?

Click here to find out for yourself. Happy reading!

ALSO BY HOPE STONE

Check out my first series of short stories which are now available in Audiobook format as well! These books can be read as stand alone stories in any order.

Book 1: Curvy Obsession (eBook) (Audiobook)
Book 2: His Obsession, Her Curves (eBook) (Audiobook Coming Soon)
Book 3: Billionaire's Party Planner (eBook) (Audiobook)
Book 4: Unforgettable Curves (eBook) (Audiobook)
Book 5: Undeniable Attraction (eBook) (Audiobook)
Book 6: Curves On Fire (eBook) (Audiobook)
Book 7: Doctors Orders (eBook)
Boxset (Books 1-3): Insta Love Alpha Males Boxset 1 (eBook) (Audiobook)
Boxset (Books 4-6): Insta Love Alpha Males Boxset 2 (eBook) (Audiobook)

CONNECT WITH HOPE

Join the Hope Stone Readers Group on Facebook. This is an exclusive group where readers and fans of drama-filled, steamy romances come together to talk about Hope's books. This is the place to engage with other fans in a fun and inclusive way as well as get access to exclusive content, find out about new releases, giveaways, and contests, as well as vote on covers before anyone else and so much more!

FREE GIFTS AND EMAIL LIST

Hey there Love,
How would you like to get FREE exclusive access to the Outlaw Souls Prequel sent directly to your inbox? Sign up for my newsletter and I will hook you up with THREE FREE eBooks, starting with the prequel followed by TWO exclusive unreleased books just for my VIP readers. You'll also be the first to hear about upcoming releases, giveaways, cover reveals, chapter reveals, and much more. Just click here, sign up and get your FREE books now!
Happy Reading,
Hope

ABOUT THE AUTHOR

Hope Stone is a contemporary romance author who loves writing hot and steamy, but also emotion-filled stories with twists and turns that keep readers guessing. Her books revolve around possessive alpha men who love protecting their sexy and sassy heroines. Discover the sweet naughtiness for yourself with guaranteed happily ever afters!

Printed in Great Britain
by Amazon